"When you left, did you know you were pregnant?" Kel asked hoarsely.

"I . . . suspected," Megan said quietly.

"Well, when were you sure? There must have come a time when you didn't have any more doubts. Maybe when you were in labor? Or when the doctor handed you the baby? Didn't it occur to you that I might like to know I was a father?"

Kel felt his rage grow. He shot to his feet, aware that the sudden movement made Megan start. *Good,* he thought savagely. *I'm glad she's afraid of me.*

After what she'd done, her fear was the least she owed him. She'd kept his child from him. His son was two years old. His name was Michael; he was big for his age.

And Kel didn't know another damned thing about him.

Dear Reader,

I just have to start telling you about this month's books with Dallas Schulze's *Michael's Father,* our American Hero title. For Kel Bryan, Megan Roarke was the answer to a heartfelt prayer—until she left him alone on the ranch, taking with her a secret that could change his life. Then it's back to Conard County with Rachel Lee's *Point of No Return,* a look inside the marriage of Nate and Marge Tate as the past returns to haunt them. Doreen Roberts sets your soul on fire in *Where There's Smoke,* while Maggie Shayne throws off enough heat to melt . . . Well, see for yourself in *Miranda's Viking.* Jo Leigh's *Suspect* matches a by-the-book cop with the most beautiful suspected murderess ever to cross his path. Finally, in *True Blue,* new author Ingrid Weaver puts her own spin on the classic tale of a good girl falling for an oh-so-bad boy.

In months to come, more excitement will be coming your way in books by authors such as Kathleen Korbel, Linda Turner, Judith Duncan and Marilyn Pappano, to name only a few of the favorite writers entertaining you every month—here in Silhouette Intimate Moments.

Enjoy!

Leslie Wainger
Senior Editor and Editorial Coordinator

Please address questions and book requests to:
Reader Service
U.S.: P.O. Box 1325, Buffalo, NY 14269
Canadian: P.O. Box 1050, Niagara Falls, Ont. L2E 7G7

AMERICAN HERO

MICHAEL'S FATHER

Dallas Schulze

Silhouette®

INTIMATE MOMENTS®

Published by Silhouette Books

America's Publisher of Contemporary Romance

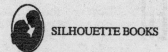

SILHOUETTE BOOKS

ISBN-0-373-07565-0

MICHAEL'S FATHER

Books by Dallas Schulze

Silhouette Intimate Moments

Moment to Moment #170
Donovan's Promise #247
The Vow #318
The Baby Bargain #377
Everything but Marriage #414
The Hell-Raiser #462
Secondhand Husband #500
Michael's Father #565

DALLAS SCHULZE

loves books, old movies, her husband and her cat—
not necessarily in that order. She's a sucker for a
happy ending, and her writing has given her an outlet
for her imagination. Dallas hopes that readers have
half as much fun with her books as she does! She has
more hobbies than there is space to list them, but is
currently working on a doll collection. Dallas loves to
hear from her readers, and you can write to her at
P.O. Box 241, Verdugo City, CA 91046.

Chapter 1

He wanted her.

That was the first thing Kel Bryan thought when he saw the blonde walk in. And it wasn't the kind of casual desire that sometimes drifted through a man's head when he saw a pretty woman, an acknowledgment of her attractiveness, the vague question of what it would be like to take her to bed. This was a gut-deep hunger of a kind he hadn't felt in a long time.

His second thought was that a woman who barely topped five feet had no business having legs that long. They were the kind of legs that made a man think of hot summer nights and cool linen sheets. The kind of legs that made him wonder how they'd feel wrapped around his waist.

Kel shifted uncomfortably in the booth and forced his gaze upward from those legs. But the change of view didn't do anything to ease the sudden snugness of his jeans. She was wearing a narrow skirt that stopped a few inches above the knee and a fitted jacket that ended just a few inches above that. The suit was a discreet pearl gray, but there was nothing discreet about the body underneath.

Kel usually liked his women on the voluptuous side, but this woman gave him a renewed appreciation for narrow hips and a small waist. Her breasts were a full rich curve. The modest neckline of her jacket exposed a triangle of creamy skin at the base of her throat, and Kel found his fingers itching to slide open the saucy brass buttons and bare more of that silky skin.

He forced his eyes away from her, aware that he was growing uncomfortably aroused. Annoyed with his reaction, he reached for his coffee and took a swallow, forgetting that the waitress had just refreshed the cup. He bit back a curse as the hot liquid scalded his tongue. The thick white cup hit the table with a thud and he reached for a glass of water to cool his burned mouth.

Maybe Colleen was right. She'd been telling him that he was spending too much time on the ranch, that he needed to get out more, meet some women. Of course, he could hardly tell his baby sister that he didn't lack for female companionship. There was a woman here in Casper whom he saw now and again when the itch got strong enough to warrant scratching. He'd been planning to give her a call once he'd finished his business today, but the idea suddenly held less appeal than it had a few minutes ago.

Then again, maybe he *should* call Carla. God knew, he was reacting like a randy teenager, getting all hot and bothered over a pair of legs. Very impressive legs, he admitted as his eyes drifted in their direction.

The blonde had stepped to one side of the doorway and opened the ridiculously small purse that swung from her shoulder to take out a mirror. Her expression was solemn and considering as she looked at her reflection. Kel could have told her that she had nothing to worry about. He guessed he'd seen more beautiful women, but she had something more than beauty. She had that indefinable something that made it hard for a man to look away once he'd seen her. He wasn't the only one, he thought, noticing the discreet and not-so-discreet looks she was receiving from half the men in the place.

Apparently satisfied with her appearance, she slipped the mirror into her purse and lifted her head to scan the restaurant. Obviously, she was meeting someone. Husband? Lover? Kel was surprised by how little he liked either possibility. He wanted to think that she was available, even if he couldn't pursue that availability. If he hadn't had other fish to fry this morning, he'd have been tempted to introduce himself and see if her attractiveness held up at close range.

But he hadn't made the trip into Casper for pleasure. He was supposed to be interviewing an applicant for the job of housekeeper at the ranch for the next few months. Considering he'd only had one applicant, he sure as hell hoped she turned out to be suitable, because he didn't have time for—

He'd been watching the leggy blonde with a sort of regretful acceptance of opportunities lost. He saw her stop one of the waitresses and ask something. The waitress was a tall woman in her mid-fifties with a brassy red beehive hairdo reminiscent of a sixties starlet. Next to her, the blonde looked as delicate as a porcelain figurine. Her hands filled with plates of ham and eggs, the waitress jerked her head toward the booths along the front of the restaurant.

The blonde looked in the direction indicated, and Kel could have sworn she looked directly at him. When she started walking toward him, he felt his stomach tighten in anticipation. Of course, several of the other booths were occupied, it wasn't necessarily his she was heading for. But Kel knew it was. He felt his mouth go a little dry as he watched her weave her way between the tables.

She was wearing heels, not so high that she teetered but just high enough to put a very interesting swing to her hips. The shoes were the same pearl gray as her suit, with a little zigzag of red leather running up the side of each pump, matching the red trim on her purse and the unexpected dots of red that were her earrings. Odd, how that little touch of color changed the gray suit from conservative to sexy.

"Mr. Bryan?" She'd stopped beside the table and was looking at him inquiringly.

"Yes." Kel slid from the booth. He loomed over her. Even in heels, she was a good foot shorter than his six four.

"I'm Megan Roarke."

Her outstretched hand disappeared inside his and Kel felt a jolt of electricity at the light touch, an awareness that went straight to his groin. From the way her blue-gray eyes widened in surprise, he knew she'd felt the same thing. The knowledge did nothing to cool his suddenly overactive libido. His fingers tightened subtly as he considered the possibility of pulling her up against his chest and satisfying his curiosity about the softness of her mouth.

God, he *had* been working too many hours.

He released her hand abruptly but resisted the urge to step back and put more distance between himself and temptation. He was damned if he'd run from a woman whose head barely reached his shirt pocket.

"Have a seat."

"Thank you."

He made the mistake of watching as she slid into the booth and felt his mouth go dry again as the movement made her skirt slide up, exposing a few more inches of slender thigh. He sat down abruptly, grateful for the shielding presence of the table.

"Would you like some coffee?" he asked politely.

"I'd prefer tea. One thing I've discovered is that Westerners tend to like their coffee a bit stronger than I'm used to."

"Good coffee should be strong enough to float a horseshoe," Kel said seriously. He lifted his hand to signal the waitress.

"Some of the stuff I've tasted could have floated a horseshoe with the horse still in it."

Her rueful smile wrinkled her nose and made Kel want to wrap his hand around the back of her neck and drag her across the table to kiss her.

"Where are you from originally?" he asked after he'd asked the beehived waitress to bring a pot of tea.

"I grew up in Minnesota but I've been doing a lot of traveling the last few years so I've lived all over the country."

"What made you come to Wyoming?"

She glanced at the waitress with a smile of thanks as the woman set her tea in front of her. The brief pause gave Kel a chance to notice the way the sunlight slanted through the window behind her and caught in her hair, making it gleam like spun moonlight. She'd caught it up in some sort of sleek bun at the back of her head, leaving just a few tendrils loose to tease her forehead and the nape of her neck. It was the sort of style that teased at a man, prim but with a touch of wildness, making him wonder how she'd look if he pulled the pins from her hair and spread it across his pillow.

"—loved the stories about outlaws and gunfighters," she was saying, and Kel realized that he'd lost the first part of her answer to his question about why she'd come to Wyoming. "I always wanted to see the country where all the stories began."

"Has it lived up to your expectations?"

"And more. It's not exactly pretty country but there's a kind of wild beauty to it that's hard to resist." As she spoke, she stacked three packets of sugar together and ripped the tops off before dumping the contents into her cup. She glanced up and saw him watching her. "I have a terrible weakness for sugar," she said with the air of someone admitting a deep character flaw.

"I have a more than passing fondness for it myself." Kel wondered if her mouth could possibly taste as sweet as it looked. Damn, but he must have been spending too much time on the ranch. With an effort, he dragged his thoughts back to the matter at hand, which was hiring a housekeeper.

"Have you ever worked as a housekeeper before?"

"Yes. I worked for a family in San Francisco two years ago." She set her spoon down and lifted her teacup, sipping the steaming liquid.

"Weren't you a little young for a housekeeper?"

"Twenty-three. I learned how to scrub a floor when I was ten so I'd had plenty of experience."

"How long did you work for them?" The tea had left a faint sheen of moisture on her mouth, and Kel had to struggle to keep his eyes off her lips and his mind on the business of conducting an interview.

"Four months."

"Do you have a reference?"

Soft color rose in Megan's cheeks and she set her cup down abruptly. "I'm afraid not."

Kel didn't say anything but simply raised his brows in question. She hesitated a moment and then shrugged.

"I had some problems with the man of the house. He seemed to feel that a housekeeper should have... duties that I didn't think were a part of the job description."

"But you stayed for four months," Kel pointed out.

"I needed the money," she said simply. "And aside from his rather clumsy attempts at seduction, I liked the job. They had two children, and I was very fond of them. I might have stayed even longer if Mr. Jefferson hadn't had too much to drink one night and decided that I'd just been playing coy and that I was really desperate to become his mistress."

There was more remembered exasperation than fear in her voice, and Kel couldn't resist asking what had happened.

"I smacked him with a frying pan."

"A frying pan?" One dark brow rose in silent comment.

"I wanted him to know I was serious," Megan said.

"Did he get the message?"

"I think so. He fired me the next morning." There was no rancor in her tone.

"You could have sued for sexual harassment," he pointed out.

Distaste twisted her mouth down on one corner. "I suppose. But it would have been hard on his wife and on the children. Besides, hitting him with a skillet was a great deal more satisfying than facing him in court."

Kel asked another question, though he knew it was a waste of time to do so. He wasn't going to hire her. He didn't need or want the temptation she provided. Running the ranch took every bit of his time and energy. The last thing he needed was to hire a long-legged blonde with hair the color of moonlight and skin like silk.

"What made you think you wanted to work as a housekeeper again?" Kel asked. "Your last experience didn't turn out so well."

"I can't imagine I'd have that kind of problem working for you, Mr. Bryan. You don't seem the type to chase your employees around the kitchen table."

Actually, Megan couldn't imagine him *having* to chase any red-blooded female around a table. The cliché tall, dark and handsome could have been invented to describe him. Over six feet of muscle and sex appeal, with hair so dark a brown that it hovered on the edge of being black. His features were strong, square-jawed and quintessentially masculine. A thick dark mustache framed his mouth. But it was his eyes that made her feel weak in the knees. Deep-set and brilliant green, they seemed to see all the way to her soul.

It was an effort to drag her attention back to the conversation.

"I'll take that as a compliment," Kel said, thinking that her confidence might be misplaced. True, he hadn't chased anyone around a table lately, but then he'd never had an employee who tempted him the way she did. Chasing Megan Roarke around a table or anywhere else didn't hold much interest, but *catching* her . . . that was a different story.

He dragged his eyes away from the soft coral of her mouth and reached for his coffee. It was time to tell her that he didn't think she'd work out—at least not as a housekeeper. If he hired her, he'd be spending the summer in a state of semiarousal. Hell, trying to ride a horse in that condition was likely to endanger his

chances of ever fathering children, he thought ruefully.

"You're not going to offer me the job, are you?"
The blunt question surprised him. It deserved an
equally blunt answer.

"No, I'm not."

That soft mouth twisted slightly and she lowered her
eyes to the table. "I'd do a good job."

"I believe you."

"But you're still not going to hire me?" She
sounded only mildly curious as she drew one fingertip through a few grains of spilled sugar on the table.

"No." Looking at the curve of her cheek and the
delicate line of her collarbone, Kel wondered how
she'd respond if he suggested that they find a motel
room and spend the rest of the afternoon in bed.

"Why not?"

It took Kel a moment to realize that she was asking
why he wasn't going to hire her to be his housekeeper,
not agreeing to spend the afternoon in bed with him.
His mouth tightened with annoyance at his wayward
thoughts.

"You're too young," he said bluntly. "And you
look as if a stiff breeze would carry you off."

"I've held my own against some pretty strong
winds," Megan said, sounding more amused than annoyed. "And I don't see what age has to do with
cleaning house."

Maybe she didn't, but he'd had in mind a more
grandmotherly type of woman. With those long legs
of hers, she'd probably manage to make mopping a
floor look like a deeply erotic activity.

"I don't think it would work." When her brows lifted in question, he reached up to run his fingers through his dark hair, looking for an excuse more acceptable than the truth, which was that he wanted her more than he could ever remember wanting a woman before. "You're hardly big enough to whip a cat," he said finally.

Megan looked surprised. "I thought you were looking for a housekeeper, Mr. Bryan, not an animal tamer."

Kel laughed despite himself but he also shook his head. "I just don't think it would work."

If I had any sense, I'd drop it, Megan thought. But she wanted this job. The moment she'd crossed the border from Utah into Wyoming, she'd felt as if she'd come home, as if the last few years of wandering had been leading here. She didn't know whether or not the feeling would last but she wanted to stay long enough to find out.

There were other jobs, of course. And money wasn't a problem, at least not for a few months. One thing about a life on the road was that it didn't cost much to maintain. She could spend the entire summer doing nothing and still have time to find work. But she didn't want to take the summer off. She wanted a job. This job.

"I guess you have enough applicants that you can afford to be choosy," she said, taking a shot in the dark.

There was a moment's pause and then Kel shook his head. "Actually, you're the only one," he admitted reluctantly.

"Then why not give me a chance?" She saw the refusal in his eyes and spoke before he could say anything. "For a week. A trial run."

"I don't know."

It wasn't exactly enthusiastic acceptance but it wasn't outright refusal, either, and Megan felt hope stir inside her. Every ounce of common sense told her to walk away, to get up, shake Kel Bryan's hand and leave. But it had been shaking hands with him the first time that had made her decide that she wanted this job. It had been like grabbing hold of a live wire and feeling sparks of electricity shoot all the way to her toes. She couldn't bring herself to just walk away from that.

"If it doesn't work out, you won't have to pay me," she said. She could hardly believe she was pressing like this. She'd never been this pushy in her life. "What have you got to lose?" she asked with a smile.

My self-control, Kel thought. *My sanity.*

He looked across the table at her. He was out of his mind to even consider it. She was trouble. All wrapped up in pale gold hair and blue-gray eyes with legs as long as sin, she was trouble in capital letters. If he hired her, he'd be spending his days semihard and aching. Either that or he'd end up taking her to bed— and break every rule in the employer-employee relations handbook, he thought ruefully.

"A week," he said, knowing he was crazy. "But I'll pay you one way or another."

"I won't arm wrestle you over it," she said, smiling.

It wasn't arm wrestling he had in mind, Kel thought. He had to be out of his mind to be agreeing to this. Of course, there was always the possibility that it was just something in the water that made her seem so attractive. Maybe when she arrived at the ranch, he'd find her no more than moderately pleasant on the eye.

And maybe pigs really did fly.

They agreed on a salary and her arrival. Since his regular housekeeper had left in a hurry to nurse her daughter through the last few months of a difficult pregnancy, Kel was glad Megan agreed to start work in a couple of days. In the two weeks since Grace Cavenaugh had left, the house had begun to show definite signs of neglect, not to mention that neither he nor Colleen was much good when it came to cooking a decent meal.

Their business concluded, Megan thanked him for the tea and slid out of the booth. Kel rose with her.

"Thank you for giving me a chance, Mr. Bryan."

"Kel. We tend to be on a first-name basis around here."

"Kel, then." She smiled up at him, a hint of shyness in her expression. "I'll see you at the Lazy B day after tomorrow."

He took the hand she thrust out, feeling the same jolt of awareness he'd felt the first time, the same urge to pull her closer. He heard her breath catch a little. The hustle and bustle of the restaurant disappeared, and for a moment it seemed as if there was just the two of them, alone on a plane of sensual awareness.

Kel's fingers shifted subtly around hers, the conventional handshake becoming almost a caress. Megan's eyes widened, suddenly more gray than blue. Her lips parted as if she was having trouble catching her breath. Kel could almost taste the softness of her mouth.

A busboy dropped a tray of dishes with a crash loud enough to shatter eardrums in half the state.

Megan jumped as if shot.

Kel dropped her hand as if it were on fire.

Each took a half step away from the other.

"I have to go," she said, her voice as breathless as if she'd just completed a marathon.

He nodded. *Had he actually been about to kiss her? Right here in front of God and half of Casper, Wyoming?* "I'll see you day after tomorrow," he said.

"Yes." Her agreement held just a touch of hesitation, and the look she shot him was uncertain. He wondered if she was having second thoughts about coming to work for him. God knew, he had second, third and fourth thoughts about hiring her, even on a trial basis. But if she'd changed her mind, she didn't say so.

"Goodbye." Her voice was a little breathless.

"Bye."

Kel watched her walk out of the restaurant, his eyes lingering on the provocative swing of her hips. She was five foot almost nothing of temptation. Pure trouble. And he'd just hired her to work on his ranch.

As Megan disappeared through the restaurant's door, he sank back into the booth. He'd lost his mind. Just having her on the place was going to cut up his peace. A week of looking at those legs, of thinking

about that pale hair spread across his pillow and he'd
be a babbling idiot.

He reached for his coffee. It wouldn't be smart to
forget that that delicate look could go along with a will
of iron. Roxanne had looked just as fragile. He hadn't
realized until after he married her that she was about
as fragile as a Brahma bull and even more dangerous.

His mouth hardened at the memory of his ex-wife.
Roxanne had been dark and several inches taller than
Megan Roarke but she'd had a similar air of delicate
femininity, the kind that tended to bring out a man's
protective instincts. Only Roxanne had proven well
able to take care of herself.

Kel rose from the booth and dropped enough money
on the table to cover the bill plus tip. He scooped his
hat off the seat and made his way to the door, nodding absently to one or two acquaintances on the way.
Standing on the sidewalk, he turned the gray Stetson
in his hands. Narrowing his eyes against the late spring
sunshine, he stared at the pay phone on the corner.

He'd been seeing Carla for a couple of years now.
She'd come out of a bad marriage with a tidy settle-
ment, payoff from her husband's wealthy Charleston
family in return for her agreement not to tell the press
that their precious son was an abusive s.o.b. She'd
moved to Wyoming, settled her two children into
school and gotten a part-time job, though she didn't
have to work.

Their informal arrangement worked out well for
both of them. He liked her, and she felt the same way
about him. But there were no ties, no strings, no
emotional entanglements. His occasional visits pro-

vided them both with a needed sexual relief without asking more of either of them than they were willing to give. Carla wouldn't mind him calling at the last minute. If she was busy, she'd say so. But if she wasn't, they could spend the rest of the morning in bed before he made the two-hour trip to the ranch.

With a muttered curse for his own stupidity, Kel shoved his hat onto his head and turned away from the phone. Striding to where he'd parked his truck, he jerked open the door and slid into the cab. He had the itch, all right, but it wasn't one Carla could scratch. The only fingers he wanted on this particular itch belonged to his new housekeeper.

Cursing himself for seven kinds of a fool, Kel headed the truck north. He was a fool not to call Carla. He was a fool to let Megan Roarke under his skin. But most of all, he was a fool to have hired her.

She was a fool to have taken the job.

Megan closed her motel room door behind her and leaned against it. She'd been a fool to push for the job. If she'd had a brain in her head, she'd have turned tail and run after that first handshake.

She stared at her hand, half expecting to see scorch marks on the palm. She could still feel the heat generated by that simple touch. Curling her fingers into her palm, Megan pushed herself away from the door and walked into the room.

Her purse bounced onto the bed as she kicked off her pumps. She sighed with pleasure and flexed her toes against the carpet. High heels were a ridiculous fashion. They were impractical, uncomfortable and clearly a remnant symbol of the days when a woman was viewed as little more than a decorative object. Which didn't explain the box in the trunk of her car that contained fifteen different pairs of them.

At five feet one and one half inches, she needed all the help she could get. Besides, cultural remnant or not, she liked the way she looked in heels. Smiling at the foolish mental argument, Megan opened the buttons on her suit jacket and shrugged out of it. Beneath it, she wore a shell-pink camisole trimmed in ivory lace.

Kel Bryan had looked at her as if he could see exactly what lay beneath her suit.

Remembering the look in those green eyes, Megan felt her cheeks warm. She'd had men look at her as if wondering what she'd look like without her clothes. No moderately attractive woman reached the age of twenty-five without getting such a look a few times. Depending on the circumstances, she'd been either annoyed or indifferent. But she'd never felt her pulse accelerate, never felt her skin heat. Never felt... aroused by a look.

Her flush deepened, and she avoided looking at her reflection in the mirror over the dresser.

The fact was, she'd never met a man who affected her the way Kel Bryan had. With a simple touch, he'd shaken her all the way to her toes, and she'd found herself all but browbeating him into giving her a job. If she'd had any sense, she wouldn't even have sat down after that first handshake. Any sensible woman would have turned and run for cover.

It wasn't too late. She didn't have to show up at the Lazy B in two days. She could pack her few belongings into her car and move on to another town—Cheyenne, maybe, or Denver. She'd never been to Colorado.

Megan sank down on the bed and stared at the dull brown carpeting under her feet. She wasn't going to Cheyenne or Denver. Day after tomorrow, she was going to make the two-hour drive north to Kel Bryan's ranch. She was going to see if his eyes were really as impossibly green as they'd seemed, if that jolt of awareness had been her imagination and if it would happen again.

It wasn't the sensible thing to do, but she'd been sensible for most of her twenty-five years and she couldn't see that it had gotten her all that much. It might be interesting to see how life went when she wasn't sensible.

Chapter 2

"If you've hired this woman to baby-sit me the way Gracie did, you're wasting your money."

Kel looked over his shoulder at his sister, Colleen, who was setting the table for breakfast.

"I think nineteen is a little old for a baby-sitter."

"I think so, too. But Gracie rarely let me out of her sight the last six months and you've been almost as bad since she left."

Kel wished he could have read some anger in her tone or expression but there was none. They could have been discussing the weather report for all the emotion Colleen revealed. A few months ago, he'd never have believed it possible that he'd actually find himself hoping for a display of temper from his usually volatile little sister.

"Gracie's known you since you were a baby. It's only natural that she'd fuss over you a bit."

"That explains Gracie. What about you?" Colleen asked, shooting him a dry look.

"I'm your older brother. I'm supposed to take care of you." He picked up an egg and started to tap it against the edge of the bowl in front of him.

"I can take care of myself, Kel. I may be crippled but I'm not helpless."

"You're not crippled!" The egg hit the bowl with more force than he'd intended. Cursing under his breath, he reached in to scoop bits of eggshell out with his fingertip.

"All right, handicapped, then."

"You're not handicapped, either!" he snapped. The eggshell dropped into the eggs and with a muttered curse he picked up the bowl and dumped the contents into the sink before turning to face his sister.

She was carrying a pitcher of orange juice from the refrigerator to the table, and Kel had to restrain a wince when he saw her awkward gait. It had been almost six months since the accident, but he couldn't get used to seeing her like this. Not Colleen, who never walked if she could run and never ran if she could ride a horse instead.

"You're not handicapped," he said again, his tone quiet but determined. "The doctor says there's no reason you shouldn't be good as new after a little more physical therapy."

"*Almost* good as new," Colleen reminded him. "I've already had four months of physical therapy and I still walk like Quasimodo."

"You'll have four more months of physical therapy and four more after that, if that's what it takes."

"I'm tired of it." She sounded like a petulant four-year-old, but at least there was some emotion in her voice.

"Tough." Kel got another egg out of the refrigerator and cracked it into the bowl. "You're not giving up, Colleen. If I have to drag you kicking and screaming to therapy, I'll do it. But you're not giving up."

"It's *my* leg."

She slammed the orange juice onto the table and Kel could feel her glaring at him. He turned to look at her. Her eyes, the same deep green as his, were bright with annoyance. But he'd rather deal with a tantrum than face the indifference with which she'd greeted almost everything these past six months. "You're right. It's your leg," he said calmly. "But I'll be damned if I'll let you give up on this."

Their eyes clashed, hers angry, his determined. Colleen looked away first.

"It hurts," she muttered, sounding so much like a little girl that it was all Kel could do to keep from snatching her up in his arms and telling her that she never had to do anything that hurt again.

"I know," he said quietly. "But it's not forever."

"It feels like it." She sighed and shrugged lightly, indifference slipping into her eyes. "I'll keep going to therapy." Her tone made it clear that she was doing it to please him, not because she believed it was doing her leg any good.

"Good." Kel didn't care why she went, just as long as she went. He turned to the neglected eggs.

A few minutes later, the two of them sat down to breakfast. Ordinarily, Kel would have been out of the house at dawn but he'd lingered this morning so that he'd be here when Megan Roarke arrived. He supposed he could have left it to Colleen to greet her, but since he'd been the one to hire her, it seemed like he should be here. At least that was the excuse he'd given himself, he admitted ruefully.

"I don't see why we couldn't have just managed on our own while Gracie was gone," Colleen said, interrupting his thoughts.

"Because I don't have time to clean house and you're not up to some of the heavier work."

"I can clean the house," she protested. "I'm not a—" She broke off, flushing as she realized what she'd been about to say.

"Cripple?" He lifted one brow as he finished the sentence for her.

"I can clean the house," she repeated, refusing to respond to his baiting look.

"What about cooking?" He picked up a slice of bacon, her contribution to the meal, and gave it a pointed look. Sooty black flakes drifted from it to his plate.

"*You* can't cook, either," she pointed out defensively, stirring her fork through the overcooked mass of scrambled eggs.

"But Megan Roarke can. At least she says she can."

Colleen considered that idea. "So you really didn't hire her to baby-sit me?"

"I hired her to keep us from starving to death." He got up from the table and picked up their barely touched plates. "It's only for a week's trial, anyway. If she can't cook or can't take the isolation, we'll be on our own again. How about hot fudge sundaes for breakfast?" he asked, peering into the freezer for something to replace the inedible breakfast.

In the two days since her interview with Kel Bryan, Megan had almost managed to convince herself that it was a desire to work in a rural setting that had prompted her to push for this job.

But rural didn't even begin to describe the ranch's setting. Isolated. Vast. Empty. She couldn't find a single word to encompass it. The land stretched out on all sides, empty except for the long ribbon of highway. To the north and west, mountains thrust upward, peaks jagged against the sky.

The turnoff for the Lazy B was marked with a simple wooden sign, and Megan turned the car onto the gravel road. A couple of miles and several cattle guards later, the road curved around the shoulder of a low hill and ended in the midst of an assortment of buildings larger than some of the towns she'd seen recently.

She stopped the car in front of a big clapboard house and turned off the engine but stayed where she was, absorbing the scene in front of her. The house was painted white, the trim deep blue. The simple colors stood out like jewels against the buff-colored hills behind it. There was a wide front porch shaded by the overhanging roof, and narrow flower beds lined the porch and the short walkway.

In front of the house was a modest-sized lawn, crisp green with summer's early growth. After the landscape she'd just driven through, the rich green seemed almost painfully bright. A low split-rail fence marked the boundary between the lawn and the packed dirt and scrubby vegetation of the ranch yard.

It was a neat, tidy picture of a well run establishment, the kind of place where it would be a pleasure to work, a perfect place to spend the summer.

But Megan stayed where she was, her palms damp on the steering wheel. There was no mistaking the tall figure who'd stepped out onto the porch.

Kel Bryan.

The one—the *only*—reason she'd pushed so hard for this job. Now that she was here, she couldn't pretend otherwise. It hadn't been working in the country that had tempted her. It had been Kel Bryan's leanly muscled body and the shock waves set off by a simple handshake.

With a feeling that fate was looking over her shoulder, Megan reached for the door handle.

Kel had almost convinced himself that he'd imagined how attractive she was, that her hair hadn't been moonlit gold, that her legs hadn't been longer than they had any right to be. When he saw her again, he'd wonder what it was that had made her seem so extraordinary.

But as she slid out of the bright blue compact, all he could think of was that her legs were even longer than he'd remembered and her hair gleamed almost silver in the bright sunlight.

One look at her and his jeans were suddenly too tight.

A week, he told himself. A week was all he'd agreed to. He could control himself for a week. She turned to shut the car door, giving him a perfect view of slender hips and a softly rounded bottom encased in faded denim that lovingly molded every curve.

Kel bit back a groan as the blood heated in his veins. She hadn't been on the property five minutes and he was ready to explode. A week in this condition and he'd end up a damned eunuch.

Megan felt her breath catch as Kel left the porch and came toward her. She'd almost convinced herself that he couldn't be as big as she'd remembered. Or as attractive. But the weakness in her knees told her that she'd been wrong. He was every bit as big, every bit as bone-meltingly good-looking as he'd been the first time they'd met.

Wearing jeans, a blue chambray shirt and a pair of scuffed black boots, he could have stepped right out of a cigarette commercial. In the sun, his dark hair had subtle red highlights, as did the thick mustache that covered his upper lip. He closed the distance between them in long, easy strides, a man comfortable with himself and his surroundings.

Megan thought about going to meet him but she wasn't entirely confident that her knees would support her. She wanted to believe that it was just nerves caused by the idea of starting a new job, but she'd never been that good at lying to herself.

"Have any trouble getting here?" Kel asked by way of greeting.

"No. The directions you gave me were very clear."

"Good." He stopped in front of her. Megan had to tilt her head to meet his eyes, those clear green eyes that had figured in her dreams these past two nights. Thinking of those dreams, she felt her color rise and hoped he'd attribute it to the warmth of the sun.

"Welcome to the Lazy B, Megan." Kel held out his hand. There was an imperceptible moment of hesitation before she placed her fingers in his. If she'd thought that remembered shock of awareness might have been her imagination, she'd been wrong.

It was like grabbing hold of a live wire, feeling the current run through her body, bringing every nerve ending to tingling life. And just as before, she saw that same awareness flare in Kel's eyes and knew he felt the spark between them.

"I wondered if you'd show up," he said abruptly.

"Are you sorry I did?" Megan was shocked to hear herself asking the question. Such bluntness wasn't like her at all. But then, this kind of sensual awareness was a new experience.

Was he sorry? Kel let his eyes drift to the soft fullness of her mouth as he debated the answer. He should be. And he very well might be later. But right now all he could think of was how her mouth would feel under his. And he knew, with unshakable certainty, that he was going to find out. Sometime before this week was up, he was going to taste Megan Roarke. He was going to have her in his arms, feel her mouth open under his and see if she tasted half as sweet as she looked.

And if she kept looking at him like that, her eyes all smoky blue, as if she was wondering the same things about him, that moment just might come a hell of a lot sooner than it should.

"I'm not sorry," he said, just when Megan had begun to think he wasn't going to answer the question. His fingers tightened over hers for an instant and then he released her and stepped back.

"Good." She could barely get the word past the knot in her throat. If she had an ounce of sense, she'd get into her car and leave this place, she thought as he turned toward the big house. But she was starting to think that she didn't have even an ounce of sense. At least not when it came to Kel Bryan.

She smelled of roses and sunshine, a soft, elusive scent that teased at the edge of his senses, making him want to move closer to discover its source. Had she dabbed perfume on the soft curve of her neck or dusted powder over her slender body when she stepped from the shower? If he were to slide open the buttons of her mint green camp shirt and bury his face in her breasts, would they smell of roses?

And even if they did, would he be able to tell with the broken nose Megan would probably give him? Kel wondered ruefully. It had been a long time since he'd found his physical responses so difficult to control. He didn't like the feeling.

He should have called Carla while he was in Casper. There was nothing mystical about his reaction to

Megan Roarke. It was caused by nothing more than a healthy sex drive. An afternoon spent in Carla's wide bed, enjoying her uninhibited response, and his fingers wouldn't be itching to loosen the neat French braid that confined Megan's hair. He'd probably hardly even notice her slender body.

Yeah, right. And if he could convince himself of that one, maybe he should try selling himself some ocean-view property in Arizona.

Megan found herself having to speed her pace to keep up with Kel as he gave her a brisk tour of the house, showing her through her new—and possibly very temporary—domain. She had the distinct feeling that he was anxious to get the tour over with. And to get away from her?

Well, he couldn't be any more anxious to part company than she was. Kel Bryan's large presence set her nerve endings ajangle, making it difficult to concentrate on what he was saying, making it difficult to think clearly at all. Once he was gone, she'd go through the house on her own and figure out where things were. At the moment, she couldn't remember whether the door he'd just shut concealed the linen closet or a bathroom.

"I think that's about it," he said.

"It's a beautiful house." That much she'd managed to absorb.

"My grandfather built it for my grandmother. She came from a wealthy Virginia family, and he wanted her to have some of the comforts she was accustomed to, even out here in the back of beyond."

"She must have been very happy here."

"Not so's you'd notice." Kel's mouth twisted in a humorless smile. "She moved back to Virginia when my father was four and never set foot west of the Mississippi again."

"It must have been difficult for your father, with parents on opposite ends of the country."

"Not really. He never saw her again. He was part of the mistake my grandmother put behind her."

"I think divorce is always hardest on the children," Megan said, remembering her own parents' divorce and the vicious quarrels that had come both before and after.

"A bad marriage is even harder."

Megan wondered if he spoke from experience. Had his parents' marriage been bad? His own? When he'd described the job to her, he'd said that he wasn't married, but that didn't mean he hadn't been in the past.

"I've got things I need to do," Kel said, glancing at his watch. "Do you have any questions?"

None that she had any right to ask. Megan shook her head.

"Colleen ought to be able to tell you anything you need to know," Kel said as they went downstairs. "Figure on four for dinner, including yourself."

Which answered the question of whether or not he expected her to eat with the family, Megan thought, watching him take a hat from the old-fashioned brass hat rack near the front door. He settled the gray Stetson on his head and turned to look at her.

Megan felt her breath catch a little as those green eyes raked over her. He looked as if he was about to say something but then changed his mind. Lifting his hand in quick farewell, he turned and left. It wasn't until he was gone that she realized she'd been holding her breath. She released it on a sigh.

"Kel tends to have that effect on people." Colleen Bryan's voice came from behind, and Megan turned to look at her.

"What effect?" she asked a little warily. *Was her attraction to the girl's brother that obvious?*

"Sort of a steamroller effect," Colleen said, limping out of the living room and into the big entryway. Kel had introduced her to his younger sister when she first arrived. She was struck again by the strong family resemblance between them. The reddish highlights in Kel's hair were deepened to a fiery auburn in his younger sister, and the stubborn set of Colleen's chin was a softer, feminine copy of her brother's iron jaw.

"Sort of a let-out-a-sigh-of-relief-when-he's-gone effect," Colleen added, stopping a few feet away.

"He is a little overwhelming," Megan agreed, though if she was honest, she'd have to admit that her sigh had been as much regret as relief.

"I bet he took you through the house at a dead run," Colleen said.

"Well . . . it was a quick tour," Megan admitted.

"Kel's not the domestic sort." Colleen's smile was friendly but there was more sadness in her eyes than any girl her age should feel.

"I guess it's a good thing he can afford to hire a housekeeper, then."

"I suppose you're wondering why *I'm* not taking over the housework and cooking while Mrs. Cavenaugh is gone this summer." There was a hint of challenge in the girl's eyes, which were the same vivid green as her brother's.

"I figured you weren't the domestic sort, either."

"Oh." Colleen's chin came down a notch. "I'm not, but I thought you might have figured it was because of this." She gestured to her left leg.

"I noticed that you limp, if that's what you're getting at."

"I don't see how you could *help* but notice it," Colleen muttered.

"But I don't have any way of knowing whether it prevents you from wielding a broom or a skillet," Megan finished calmly. "Does it?"

"No. Well, not much, anyway," the girl amended. "Kel doesn't think I can do the heavier stuff. Besides, I think he wants you to keep an eye on me, the way Gracie, our old housekeeper, did." There was both challenge and uncertainty in her look, and Megan felt her heart break just a little for all that youthful pride.

"If that's what your brother had in mind, he didn't say anything about it to me," she said, glad she could speak honestly. "As far as I know, I'm just here to cook and clean house. And I'm here on a trial basis, even for that. You look a little too old to require a baby-sitter."

"That's what Kel said when I asked him. He said he just wanted to make sure we didn't starve to death. I'm not much good in the kitchen, either," Colleen admitted. "I've spent a lot more time on a horse than I have at a stove."

"Well, I know considerably more about stoves than I do about horses, so that makes us even." Megan glanced at her watch and saw that it was a little past noon. "Why don't I start earning my salary by making us both some lunch? Maybe you could keep me company and fill me in on anything your brother might have forgotten."

Colleen hesitated a moment before nodding, and Megan was reminded of a half-wild kitten, wanting to make friends but skittish about the process.

Colleen sat down at the kitchen table, and Megan pretended not to hear her stifled sigh of relief as she took the weight off her leg. Kel's tour of the kitchen had consisted of stepping through the door long enough to confirm that it was indeed the room he'd claimed. It would take a while to figure out where everything was, but for the moment she found everything she needed in the big refrigerator. With the ingredients for a salad lined up on the counter in front of her, Megan glanced over her shoulder to find Colleen watching her.

"What happened to your leg?" she asked, deciding that it was better to get the subject out in the open rather than skirt around its edges for the next week.

"A riding accident." Colleen looked startled but not offended. "It was broken in three places. I was out on the range and it took a while to get help."

"Were you alone?" Turning to get the salt and pepper shakers, Megan saw the girl flush and then pale, her pretty mouth tightening a little as she looked down at the table.

"No. I wasn't alone."

Something in her tone told Megan that she'd touched a sore point. Odd that the accident itself didn't seem to be taboo, but her companion was. She wondered if she'd be on the Lazy B long enough to find out the whole story.

"How long ago was the accident?" She slivered some ham and scattered it over the top of the lettuce.

"Six months. And I still walk like Toulouse-Lautrec."

Megan chuckled at the description, and after a startled moment Colleen smiled sheepishly. Megan was willing to bet that no one on the Lazy B had dared to laugh at the girl's dramatic description.

"You're too tall to be Toulouse-Lautrec," she said as she brought the bowls of salad to the table and set them down. "And I don't think you're tall enough to be Ken Curtis."

"Who's Ken Curtis?"

"On *Gunsmoke*. He was a deputy or something and he limped. Or was it Dennis Weaver who limped?" Megan frowned, trying to remember. "It doesn't matter," she said, shrugging. "I think you're too short to be either one of them. What would you like to drink?"

"There's some iced tea in the green pitcher," Colleen said. She watched Megan take the plastic pitcher out and fill two glasses. "Aren't you uncomfortable? Talking about my leg, I mean?" she asked, sounding a little bewildered and very young.

"Should I be?" Megan sat down and looked at the girl across the oak table.

"Everyone else is. They just tell me that I'm going to get better."

"Are you?"

"I...don't know." Colleen sighed and looked at her leg as if she might be able to read the answer there. "Maybe..."

She let her voice trail off, and Megan was surprised by the urge to put her arms around the girl and tell her that of course everything was going to be all right. Good grief, what was it about the Bryan family that they brought out such strong reactions in her?

"Well, as long as it's still a maybe, it seems a little soon to be giving up, don't you think?" She kept her voice brisk, sensing that Colleen had had more than enough sympathy.

"That's what they keep saying," Colleen muttered.

"Maybe you should believe them."

"Maybe." The word sounded a little less doubtful this time. The girl looked at Megan, her emerald eyes surprised and curious. "I don't know why I'm talking to you about this. I bite Kel's head off every time he brings it up."

"Sometimes it's easier to talk to a stranger."

"I guess." Colleen picked up her fork and poked absently through the salad. "Kel worries a lot. And he fusses at me. You know how family is."

Megan gave what she hoped was an understanding smile. No, actually, she didn't know how family was. Not the kind of family Colleen was talking about. She couldn't remember her parents or her grandparents ever worrying about her, other than to worry about who was going to get stuck taking care of her. It must be nice to have someone fuss at you, she thought wistfully.

"Do you have any brothers or sisters?" Colleen asked.

"I'm an only child." And a good thing, too. Her grandparents had been reluctant enough about rearing one grandchild. Heaven knew what they'd have done if her mother had dumped two children on their doorstep.

The conversation moved on to other, less personal topics, and by the end of the meal, they'd established the beginnings of a friendship. Colleen's physical therapist arrived soon after lunch, and she and Colleen disappeared into the sun room for a session of torture—at least that was Colleen's description.

Megan spent some time unpacking in the room Kel had said was hers. She could enjoy spending a summer here, she thought, looking out one of the big multipaned windows that made the room seem bigger than it was. Rolling hills and scrubby vegetation stretched as far as the eye could see. It wasn't a pretty landscape and it lacked the deep green beauty of the Minnesota woods that had bordered her grandparents' farm.

She'd lived there from the time she was eight until she left home at eighteen, and the woods had been her sanctuary, a place where she felt welcomed in a way she'd never been in the tidy little farmhouse.

Certainly this was a very different landscape, but she fancied she felt a similar acceptance, a feeling of homecoming. Oh, yes, she could be happy here, if she got a chance to stay.

Her gaze sharpened as a black horse cantered around the side of the house. There might be any number of men on the ranch who wore a gray Stetson and whose shoulders filled out a blue chambray shirt. The rider didn't *have* to be Kel Bryan. It wasn't reasonable to assume that it was. But her pulse was suddenly beating faster and she felt breathless. And reasonable or not, she knew exactly who it was astride the big black horse.

As if sensing her gaze, he tilted his head and looked directly at her. His hat shadowed his eyes, but Megan could feel them raking over her, leaving tingling awareness in their wake. She told herself to step back from the window, maybe give him a casual wave first. But she stayed where she was, incapable of movement.

The moment seemed to stretch forever but it could only have been a matter of seconds before Kel looked away, giving some subtle signal to the horse that sent it cantering away from the house. Megan watched him go, feeling as if she'd just run a race in hundred-degree weather, all breathless and weak-kneed.

Chapter 3

Colleen helped with the dinner preparations, mostly by pointing out where things were and saving Megan the trouble of constantly searching through the cupboards. Just as she had at lunch, Megan found the girl pleasant company. She had the impression that Colleen didn't go out much, and it wasn't hard to guess that it was because of the injury to her leg. No doubt the limp made her feel conspicuous, and at nineteen it would seem much easier to hide away than to tough out the inevitable curious looks. But the isolation was lonely.

Well, no one knew better than she did what it was to be lonely and hungry for someone to talk to. She'd spent most of her childhood perfecting those emotions, she thought ruefully. The memory warmed her response to Colleen, and by the time dinner was on the table, Colleen was talking as if they'd known each other for years rather than hours.

Kel walked into the kitchen and found his sister and his new housekeeper laughing together. He stopped just inside the doorway, struck by two things at once. The first was that he hadn't heard Colleen laugh nearly often enough these past months. The second was that Megan Roarke seemed to grow more attractive every time he saw her.

She'd been stirring something on the stove but, as if feeling his gaze, she turned toward him. Their eyes clashed across the big kitchen. She was flushed from the heat of whatever she was cooking—and whatever it was smelled damned good, he noticed absently. The French braid that held her hair was a little less neat than it had been when she arrived. Soft tendrils of moonlight-colored hair had slipped loose to curl against her forehead and neck. There was a smudge of flour on her cheek, a smattering of tomato sauce on the plain white apron she'd wrapped around her slender waist, not a trace of lipstick on her soft mouth.

And it took every ounce of self-control he possessed to keep from walking across the kitchen to drag her into his arms and kiss her senseless.

"Kel." Colleen's voice held more life than he'd heard in weeks. "Megan made spaghetti for dinner and homemade French bread."

"You made bread?" So that was part of what he'd been smelling, he thought, his eyes finding the towel-wrapped loaves on the counter.

"You can't have spaghetti without garlic toast," she said. Her voice was a little breathless, and he wondered if it was because she'd been working or because her pulse was as erratic as his.

"There's plenty of bread in the freezer," he said. He'd been holding his hat, and now he set it on one of the hooks next to the door. He reached up to run his fingers through his hair, ruffling it into thick dark waves.

"It's not the same as fresh."

He studied her for a moment and then his mouth curved in a slow smile. "Rolling out the big guns early?"

Megan widened her eyes innocently, but he saw the laughter in them and knew she understood his question. She was out to persuade him to keep her on after the trial week was up and she wasn't above using homemade bread as a bribe.

"Don't you like fresh bread?"

"Yeah, I like it." Worse, he was starting to think he might like her, too.

Kel became aware of his little sister's curious gaze darting back and forth between the two of them and he quickly subdued the lingering trace of a smile as he went to the sink to wash his hands. He sometimes forgot that Colleen was not a little girl anymore. She was definitely old enough to pick up on any hint of something personal going on between her brother and the new housekeeper.

Megan turned to the stove and gave the spaghetti sauce a quick stir, aware that her fingers were not quite steady. Kel Bryan was one potent hunk of male pulchritude. In fact she'd never met a more pulchritudinous man in her life. But just because he set butterflies aflutter in her stomach, that didn't mean she had to lose control of the situation.

If only she knew what the situation was.

The fourth person at dinner turned out to be a friend of the family named Gun Larsen. According to Kel's introduction, Gun was working on the Lazy B for the summer. Megan couldn't remember ever being in the same room with so much pure masculine beauty—or so much sheer size, she added, looking from one man to the other. Was it something in the Wyoming water that caused men to grow to the size of redwoods? Or had she just stumbled into the land of the giants?

Gun matched Kel inch for inch in height. She wouldn't have thought it possible but his shoulders were even broader and his hands looked big enough to crush granite boulders like cream puffs. But the resemblance between the two men ended with their size. Gun's hair was the color of just ripened wheat and his eyes were a clear, laughing blue.

"You're much prettier than Gracie," Gun said by way of greeting.

"Thank you." Megan's hand disappeared in his, her eyes widening as she took in the classic perfection of his features. The man could have posed for a statue of Adonis, she thought, momentarily struck dumb. But she felt none of the electricity when she shook his hand that she felt just glancing at Kel. She admired Gun's looks—what living, breathing woman wouldn't?—but admiration was all she felt.

"It's about time Kel found someone to take over while Gracie's off taking care of her daughter," Gun said as he released her hand. "We were all in danger of starving to death."

"I can see you're down to skin and bones." Megan eyed the width of his shoulders and wondered if she should add another box of spaghetti to the pot.

Gun's appreciative grin faded as his eyes went over her head to Colleen, who'd just come into the dining room. Something flashed in his eyes, a look Megan couldn't quite identify. Pain? Regret? It was gone too quickly to be sure. Megan turned to look at the girl, seeing all the animation gone from her face, leaving her features stiff.

"Hello, Colleen."

"Gun." Colleen mumbled his name by way of greeting, her eyes sliding across him without pausing.

"How are you?"

"Fine." Colleen's fingers tightened around the stack of plates she was carrying until the knuckles turned white, and Megan half expected to see the china crack. "I'll just go check the spaghetti," she said, when the silence threatened to stretch. She thrust the plates at Megan and turned to hurry from the room, her gait made more awkward by her quick pace.

Megan turned to set the plates on the table, her eyes skimming across Gun Larsen's face as she did so. There was no mistaking the bleak look in his eyes. Whatever the reason for Colleen's reaction to him, it had cut him deeply.

After the little scene, she was unsurprised when Colleen was almost silent during dinner, her eyes rarely leaving her plate. The men's discussion of ranching business served to cover her silence but Megan doubted she was the only one who noticed it. Her curiosity was piqued. If Colleen had been older or Gun younger, she might have suspected a broken love affair. But Gun seemed about the same age as Kel, thirty-five or -six, and she couldn't see Kel tolerating any kind of affair between his nineteen-year-old sister and his friend.

Megan wondered if she'd be here long enough to find out what the situation was.

Colleen excused herself almost immediately after dinner, saying she was tired, but Megan would have bet her next week's salary that the girl's departure had less to do with courting Morpheus than it did with avoiding Gun.

She pondered that thought while she cleaned up the kitchen. The two men had gone down to the barn to check on a mare that was due to foal any day. But they'd both complimented her on the meal before they left. Not that they'd needed to say anything. The fact that each had consumed two huge helpings of spaghetti and meatballs was compliment enough.

She could grow to like it here, Megan thought as she shut the dishwasher. She delayed turning it on a moment, savoring the absolute quiet of the big old house. No traffic, no neighbor's television or radio, nothing but the rusty sound of crickets scratching out their song.

Her mouth curving in a soft smile, she flipped the switch and the quiet vanished in the hum of the dishwasher. She wanted this job and it wasn't only because of her attraction to Kel Bryan, though she couldn't deny that that had been the driving motivation. She needed what the ranch had to offer—peace and quiet, a chance to hear herself think, time to figure out where her life was going.

With the kitchen immaculate, Megan wandered through the dining room and into the entryway. She was tired and it wasn't too early to consider going up to her room. A nice warm bath and a good night's sleep sounded lovely. But instead of going upstairs, she pushed open the screen door and stepped out onto the wide front porch.

Letting the door close quietly behind her, she drew in a deep breath. As she released it, she felt as if she was letting go of all the tensions that seemed a normal part of city living. She'd spent the last year in Los Angeles, long enough for the acrid bite of smog to begin to seem normal.

Megan closed her eyes to savor the absence of carbon monoxide. She'd never really appreciated that clean air could have a taste, too. It tasted of mountain springs and tall grass, of sagebrush and cottonwood, of wide open space and endless skies.

"It's something, isn't it?"

Startled, Megan opened her eyes to see Gun standing on the ground below where she leaned on the porch railing. "I didn't hear you," she said.

"Sorry. I'll try to walk harder."

"I guess I'm so used to city noises that anything less than a blaring horn just doesn't register," she said, smiling. "I thought you were checking on a mare."

"She decided to wait another day or two." Gun climbed the steps to join her on the porch. It struck Megan that, for such a big man, he was very light on his feet. "Kel will be up in a bit," he added, seeing her eyes go past him.

Megan gave what she hoped was a disinterested shrug, as if Kel Bryan's whereabouts were of absolutely no interest to her. She only wished it was true.

"Are you from this area?" she asked.

"Born and raised a few miles north of here," he said, nodding his head in that direction. "My father's ranch borders the Bryan place."

Megan opened her mouth to ask why he was spending the summer working on the Lazy B when his father owned the neighboring ranch, then closed it without speaking. It was none of her business.

"My father and I don't see eye to eye," Gun said, apparently reading her mind. "Actually, last time we saw each other, he promised to greet me with a shotgun if I ever set foot on his land again."

His tone was light but Megan couldn't help but think that there was an underlying note of pain in the words. Or maybe it was just reflecting old hurts of her own onto Gun. All the years she'd wondered what she'd done to cause her parents to walk away from her. It was only in the past few years that she'd finally realized there wasn't anything an eight-year-old could do to deserve abandonment, that it wasn't what she'd done, it was simply what her parents had been.

"Family's never as simple as *The Brady Bunch* made it look," she said ruefully.

"Too bad. Just think how great it would be if every problem could be solved in half an hour with time left over for commercials."

"And your biggest problem was whether your dad would loan you the car to go to the big dance."

Gun chuckled. "Or whether your burgundy leisure suit would be ready in time to pick up your date."

"Now there was a big problem."

Kel saw them laughing together as he came up from the barn and he slowed. They made an attractive couple. Gun lowered his head to hear what Megan was saying and the porch haloed their fair hair, reminding Kel of the illustrations of angels in childhood picture books.

Or Ken and Barbie, he thought irritably.

His footsteps were heavier than they needed to be on the porch steps and he was unreasonably pleased when their laughter trailed off. Not that it mattered who Megan laughed with. He sure as hell didn't care. It was just that it was late and he was tired and the two of them standing there laughing like a pair of idiots grated on his nerves.

"We were just discussing *The Brady Bunch* as a model for problem solving," Gun said, turning as Kel stepped onto the porch.

"*The Brady Bunch?*" They were discussing a twenty-year-old television show?

"Sure. The show offered a microcosm of life experience," Gun said, drawing his face into solemn lines. "I think it should be considered on a par with groundbreaking social commentary programs like *Leave it To Beaver* and *Life With Father.*"

"Let's not forget *The Three Stooges,*" Kel said dryly. "Now *there* was a show filled with deeper meaning."

"Clearly a statement against the meaningless violence of society." Gun shook his head, drawing his mouth down in a reasonable semblance of professorial concern.

"I always wanted to be able to twitch my nose like Samantha on *Bewitched,*" Megan said, sounding wistful.

"A woman as beautiful as you are doesn't need to twitch her nose to be bewitching," Gun said with such obvious gallantry that Megan grinned.

"Flattery like that could get you any number of things," she said lightly.

"I'd settle for another slice of that pecan pie you made for dinner."

Megan chuckled, a soft warm sound that made Kel want to see if it tasted as good as it sounded. And Gun was the one who'd made her laugh. Not that it meant anything. Charm came to Gun as naturally as breathing, a fact that had never bothered Kel in the past. But it bothered him now.

"I think there's a couple of slices left over," Megan said. She straightened away from the railing as if to go into the house and cut the pie. Gun would go with her, and unless he wanted to trail along like a lost calf, the two of them would be alone in the kitchen.

"It's getting late," he said abruptly.

Gun and Megan turned to look at him, their expressions faintly surprised. *As if one of the posts had spoken up,* Kel thought sourly.

"Not quite time to turn into a pumpkin," Gun commented.

"Workdays start early on a ranch," Kel said, addressing the comment to Megan, speaking as employer to employee. "You probably have things to do before you turn in." He ignored the knowing grin that appeared on Gun's face.

Actually, she didn't have much to do but Megan knew a dismissal when she heard one. She flushed a little, wondering if she was being gently reminded that she was the housekeeper and shouldn't be fraternizing with a friend of the family. Kel hadn't struck her as being the sort who'd care about such things but snobbery turned up in odd places.

"Now that I think about it, it is getting late," Gun said. "Maybe I'll have a piece of that pie for breakfast in the morning."

"I'm not sure pecan pie qualifies as a healthy start to your day." Megan smiled at him.

"Breakfast isn't part of your job," Kel reminded her before Gun could say anything.

Gun's grin grew even wider and he shot Kel a look she couldn't interpret. "I can probably manage to cut myself a slice of pie," he said.

"I thought you could." Kel looked at him, green eyes clashing with blue.

Megan felt as if she'd come in on the middle of a movie and had missed some vital piece of information. There seemed to be something going on between the two men but she hadn't the faintest idea what it was. Perhaps it was one of those strange masculine rituals that women simply weren't primitive enough to understand.

"I think I will go up," she said. She said good-night to both men and went inside.

She actually was rather tired, Megan thought. A warm bath sounded like heaven. Then she could crawl under the covers and read for a little while. She'd bought a history of Wyoming while she was in Casper and she was looking forward to reading more about this place that felt so strangely like home to her.

Before going upstairs, she went to the kitchen, checking to be sure that the meat for tomorrow night's dinner was thawing in the refrigerator. As Kel had so pointedly told Gun, each person was on his own for breakfast. At lunch, the men generally ate with the hands so she only had to worry about feeding herself and Colleen. Dinner was the only meal Kel would be sharing with them on a regular basis. Which was probably just as well, she thought ruefully. Considering the effect he had on her nervous system, his presence could wreak havoc on her digestion.

Satisfied that the kitchen was in order for the next day, she snapped off the light and left the room. Her foot was on the bottom stair when she heard the door open behind her. A shiver of awareness ran down her spine even before she turned and met Kel's eyes. He wasn't close enough for her to read his expression and she sincerely hoped that his eyesight wasn't sharper than hers. If it was, she was afraid he might be able to see the way her knees weakened at the sight of him.

"I was just going up to bed," she said, feeling the need to fill the silence.

"I think I'll join you."

Megan forgot how to breathe. *Join her? In bed?* She felt her eyes widen as she stared at him.

"Join me?" she repeated, her voice only a little higher than normal.

"Going upstairs," he clarified as he pushed the door shut behind him. A downward sweep of his palm turned off the porch light. "I think I'll turn in, too."

"Oh." *Of course that was what he'd meant,* she scolded herself. *And that was relief she felt, not disappointment. Not even for a moment did she feel disappointed.*

"You didn't lock the door," she pointed out.

"There aren't very many thieves motivated enough to drive this far off the highway to find something to steal." He reached just inside the living room door to shut off the lamp. "Besides, they'd have to drive right by the bunkhouse and Gun sleeps like a cat."

"Gun sleeps in the bunkhouse?" she asked, trying to keep her breathing steady as Kel crossed the oak floor toward her.

"He prefers it," Kel answered shortly.

"Oh." She seemed to be saying that a lot lately but it was as much as she was capable of at the moment.

Kel stopped in front of her, close enough for her to see the clear green of his eyes. She was standing on the bottom step, which put them almost at eye level. If she leaned forward just a little . . .

Her eyes were smoke and twilight, Kel thought, pale blue rimmed with darker gray. He let his gaze drift downward, lingering on the soft coral of her mouth before finding the pulse that beat a little too quickly at the base of her throat. He wanted to put his mouth against that pulse, to taste the flutter of her heartbeat. From there, it would be easy to let his mouth slide down the open collar of her shirt.

He saw the movement of her throat as she swallowed, and it took considerable self-control to force his eyes to her face. He only had to lean forward a little to find out if her mouth could possibly taste as sweet as it looked.

Her lips parted as if she was having trouble getting enough air.

So close.

She turned suddenly and started up the stairs. Kel stayed where he was for a moment, his hand clenched over the newel post, his breathing just a little ragged. Damn, but he couldn't remember the last time a woman had affected him this way. Not even his ex-wife, and he'd wanted her enough to convince himself that what he was feeling was love.

If Megan hadn't turned away, he would have kissed her. And from kissing her, it wouldn't have taken more than a half step to find himself making love to her on the damn stairs like a sex-crazed maniac. Even more annoying was the fact that, rather than being grateful that he'd been prevented from making a total fool of himself, he was disappointed.

Damn.

His long legs made short work of the stairs and he caught up with Megan as she reached the second floor. The look she gave him was both wary and aware. He could understand both feelings, he thought ruefully.

He saw her glance in the direction of Colleen's room and knew she was thinking that his room was probably on the same side of the house. He nodded in the opposite direction and saw her eyes widen as she realized that the room he'd given her had to be near his own. He waited for her to say something—a protest? A warning about nocturnal wanderings? But she simply turned and walked down the hallway.

She smelled of fresh bread and flowers, he thought. A strangely erotic combination. But he was starting to think that just about everything about Megan Roarke was erotic—or seemed so to him. He was also starting to wish he hadn't given in to the impulse to put her on this side of the house. There was a perfectly good guest bedroom next to Colleen's room. How the hell was he supposed to sleep knowing that she was right across the hall?

His room was right across the hall from hers? Megan felt her heart thump against her breastbone when Kel pushed open the door. She caught a glimpse of smooth oak floors and the corner of a peeled post bed.

"That's...your room?" she asked, hoping he wouldn't notice the odd little break in her voice.

"Uh-huh." He nodded, his eyes going over her in a look reminiscent of the one the big bad wolf must have given Little Red Riding Hood right before gulping her down, red cape and all. "If you need anything, just give a whistle."

The offer might have been tongue-in-cheek but the look in his eyes said he wouldn't have any objection if she took him up on it.

"I, ah, doubt I'll need anything." Her voice shook and she swallowed to steady it. "Good night."

"Good night."

How was it possible for him to send shivers down her spine with even the most prosaic of words? she wondered despairingly. Megan felt those green eyes watching her as she pushed open her door.

She couldn't resist the urge to glance at him as she stepped into her room. Their eyes met for an instant and she thought it was almost possible to see the electricity that arced between them.

And then she shut the door and leaned against it, her knees as weak as if she'd just climbed twenty flights of stairs.

Chapter 4

Kel had heard it said that you should never marry someone until you'd seen them first thing in the morning, before they'd had their first cup of coffee. He understood the thinking. If you woke up slowly, it would be wise to know if you were about to make a lifetime commitment to someone who bounded from bed singing the joys of the day.

Colleen had been known to threaten dismemberment for anyone foolish enough to smile at her before she'd been up at least an hour. His ex-wife had rarely left their bed much before noon, only one of many ways in which she'd failed to make the adjustment to ranch life.

Ranching tended to make a morning person out of even the most confirmed night owl. There was simply too much to be done to allow precious daylight hours to slip by. Getting up at dawn was normal for him, but he hadn't expected his new housekeeper to do the same.

Kel was mixing eggs and milk into a bowl of pancake mix when Megan entered the kitchen. He looked up, his first reaction surprise, his second the surge of hunger that was rapidly becoming familiar. It was the first time he'd seen her with her hair loose. She'd caught it back from her face with a pair of tortoiseshell combs and then let it fall in pale gold waves to just below her shoulders. He had the immediate urge to slide his fingers through it, to see if it was as soft as it looked.

"Good morning." A faint, sleepy huskiness lingered in her voice.

"'Morning. There's coffee," he added, nodding to the coffeemaker.

"Is there a horse in it?" she asked.

"A horse?" His eyebrows climbed in question. Then he remembered their first conversation about how strong Westerners liked their coffee. He grinned. "Barely strong enough to float a small horseshoe," he told her.

"Not much reassurance." But she took a cup from the wooden cup rack that sat beside the coffeemaker. Megan's delicate shudder as she sipped the thick black brew made Kel's smile widen.

"This tastes like there's a horse actually in it," she muttered.

"Cream in the fridge," he suggested as he finished stirring the pancake batter. "You want some pancakes?"

"I'm supposed to be the one cooking for you," Megan said as she took the carton of cream from the refrigerator.

"Not breakfast." He flicked water onto the big cast-iron griddle that rested across two of the stove's burners. The droplets sizzled and bounced, vanishing in a heartbeat. "There's plenty of batter."

"Okay. I usually make do with toast and tea. I haven't had pancakes in ages." He was aware of her watching him as he used a measuring cup to dip batter onto the hot griddle.

"Ranch breakfasts tend to be on the hearty side," he said, nodding his head to where half a dozen sausages sizzled on another burner. "It's a long time between now and lunch."

"Colleen said you couldn't cook," Megan commented, watching as he flipped the pancakes at just the right moment.

"I can't. But Aunt Jemima does a fine job." He nodded to the box. "And frying a sausage doesn't take much skill. But you don't want to see what I can do to an egg."

"Bad?"

"Criminal."

"I've been known to fry a respectable egg," she said, her eyes smiling at him over the rim of her coffee cup. "How about tomorrow morning I return the favor and cook you breakfast?"

"That's not part of your job," he reminded her.

"But since this is a trial week, I should do my best to impress, don't you think?"

If she only knew! She'd already made quite an impression, he thought as she turned to get out a plate and silverware for herself. Kel found his eyes drifting over her slender curves. She was wearing a plain cotton shirt the exact color of raspberry sherbet. It was tucked into a pair of softly worn jeans and he wanted nothing more than to put his hands around her waist and pull her close to him.

"Is something burning?" Megan turned, plate in hand, her short straight nose wrinkled, her eyes questioning.

"Damn!" Kel turned and began quickly scooping the pancakes off the griddle. The undersides were considerably beyond done. Irritated with himself, he stacked them on a plate to be thrown out. "Good thing I made plenty of batter," he muttered.

If I could just keep my mind on the pancakes and off Megan Roarke, I'd be doing all right.

The rest of the pancakes turned out golden brown and perfect. Since Kel watched them as carefully as a chef hovering over a pan of hollandaise sauce, they didn't have a chance to do otherwise. Megan poured juice for both of them, adding, at his request, a tall glass of milk for Kel. She tried not to think of what a perfect domestic picture they would have presented to anyone who happened to be watching.

She asked Kel what kind of work he'd be doing that day, and as she listened to him talk about moving cattle on to summer range, she thought how nice it would be to have a home of her own and a man of her own to sit across the table from. To talk about what the day would hold, to make plans for the future with, to dream with.

She'd had the dream since she was a child, and it didn't take a therapist to tell her that it was at least partially a reaction to the circumstances of her own childhood. She'd never known anything remotely approaching the kind of idyllic family life in her fantasy.

When they'd finished eating, she insisted that she'd do the cleanup. Kel, with a glance out the window to where the pale light of dawn was giving way to golden sunshine, agreed. He'd already lingered longer over the meal than he normally did.

"Breakfast tomorrow is my treat," Megan reminded him as she stacked their plates and carried them to the counter.

"Right." Just looking at her across a breakfast table was a treat, he thought, his eyes drifting over her. In that raspberry-colored shirt, with her pale hair curling onto her shoulders, she looked downright edible. He supposed it was a little too early in their relationship for him to suggest that she forget the bacon and eggs and offer herself as a main course.

Kel turned away before the urge to suggest just that became overwhelming.

Megan leaned against the counter to watch Kel stride across the packed dirt of the ranch yard. It ought to be illegal for a man to be that attractive, especially first thing in the morning before she'd had a chance to get her defenses in order. Not that she was sure there *was* any defense. How did she go about convincing her pulse not to beat double time whenever she saw him?

Kel disappeared into the barn and she turned away from the window with a sigh. She was here to take care of his house, not to fall in love with the man. She only hoped her heart didn't forget that.

Her first full day on the Lazy B set the pattern for the week that followed. After breakfast, she tidied the kitchen, decided what to make for lunch and dinner, then went to work on the rest of the house. The house was large but not difficult to care for and she had plenty of free time.

She and Colleen shared lunch and then spent most of the afternoon together. Megan sensed a loneliness in the girl and suspected it might be a recent development. She couldn't quite imagine such a bright, pretty young woman not having plenty of friends. Perhaps, after the accident that had injured her leg, Colleen had withdrawn. An understandable reaction, particularly for a nineteen-year-old.

Whatever the cause of her loneliness, it was a feeling to which Megan could easily relate. Shy, introverted bookworms made few friends, and it had always been so much easier to lose herself in a book than to risk the almost inevitable rejection she'd get from other, more active children—children whose parents actually wanted them.

Gun joined the Bryans for dinner each night, and the tension between him and Colleen remained the same as it had been that first night. Megan wondered at its source but didn't feel as if she knew Colleen well enough yet to probe for answers. If Kel let her stay past this trial week . . .

If she didn't have the good sense to leave on her own before she risked a broken heart . . .

Two big ifs, she thought ruefully as the end of the trial week neared. She liked it here, liked the work, liked the quiet, liked the sense of family that lingered in the big house.

And liked Kel Bryan more than was wise.

There was a danger in that. She could end up hurt if she stayed. But she knew that, if he asked her, she wouldn't be able to say no.

At the end of the agreed-upon trial period, Kel sat in his study waiting for Megan to join him when she was done tidying up after dinner. When he'd said he'd like to talk with her, she'd given him a wary look before murmuring her agreement. Colleen had given Megan an encouraging look and thrown a warning glance in his direction. He'd already had an earful from his little sister, who seemed to think Megan's continued presence was a foregone conclusion.

Gun, who knew all about the trial period, had given Megan a discreet thumbs-up as he left. The memory made Kel frown. His friend's easy charm had never bothered him before, but he found it irritating when that charm was directed toward Megan. The feeling came perilously close to jealousy, which should be reason enough for him to give her a check and send her on her way.

Kel frowned at the brightly lit computer screen. He was supposedly updating records on some breeding experiments he was running, but his mind kept wandering. In a few minutes, Megan was going to walk in here, expecting him to tell her whether or not she had a job for the summer.

By all reasonable criteria, there could be only one answer. She'd proven herself more than capable of the job. The house was clean enough to pass even Grace Cavenaugh's critical eye, and when it came to cooking, Megan's style was a little more exotic than Gracie's, but if he had a complaint, it was that he was eating too much.

And she'd been good for Colleen. His little sister was happier than she'd been since the accident. She'd been downright insistent that Megan stay on, which was more interest than she'd shown in anything else these past few months. That fact alone ought to be enough to insure Megan the job.

So why was he hesitating?

The cursor seemed to be blinking faster, as if impatient with his inaction. With a muttered curse, Kel exited the program and turned the computer off. In the resulting silence, he could hear the steady ticking of the clock on the fireplace mantel. It sounded as impatient with his indecision as the cursor had been. *She's perfect for the job. And she was the only applicant. If you let her go, you're going to be back to frozen dinners, burned steaks and dirty clothes.*

Yeah, but maybe he'd be able to go to sleep at night without staring at the ceiling while his imagination presented an endless series of pictures as to what Megan might—or might not—be wearing to bed.

Thoughts that had done little to ensure him a decent night's sleep.

So let her stay and let what happens happen.

As if he didn't know exactly what would happen. Restless, he stood up and moved to the window. Pulling aside the coffee-colored drapes, Kel stared out into the darkness.

If Megan Roarke stayed, they were going to end up in bed together.

He'd be lying to himself if he pretended otherwise. And she'd be lying to herself if she didn't admit the same. The awareness between them was too strong to be ignored. It was there whenever they were together. She felt it, too. He could see it in her eyes, those wide blue-gray eyes that were starting to haunt a great deal more of his thoughts than he liked.

So what if you sleep with her? You're both adults. There's nothing wrong with an affair. It would be no different from sleeping with Carla.

Except that he'd already spent more time thinking about Megan in the week since they'd met than he'd spent thinking of Carla in the three years he'd been seeing her. That should have been a warning. He'd married the last woman who'd lingered in his thoughts like that, and look what a disaster that had been.

Roxanne had envisioned life as a successful rancher's wife being a series of luncheons, dinners and perhaps an occasional masked ball. Kel's mouth twisted bitterly as he remembered her horrified expression when she'd realized how isolated the ranch was. She'd apparently pictured something along the lines of a Kentucky bluegrass country horse farm, with neat green fields, picturesque white fences and plenty of opportunities for her to exercise her talents as a hostess. A Fourth of July barbecue had not been what she had in mind.

He'd been fortunate that, while on a trip to Boston to visit her family, Roxanne had met a wealthy businessman twenty-five years her senior who was looking for exactly what she had to offer. Since she was marrying into more money than even she could imagine spending, she'd forgone her right to a piece of the ranch, simply dusted the Wyoming dirt from her dainty heels and departed for points east.

Their marriage had lasted a year, and Kel doubted it would have lasted that long except that they were undeniably compatible in the bedroom. But by the time they'd divorced, even that compatibility had worn thin. He hadn't been sorry to see her go, but he'd been bitterly angry with himself for being such a fool.

The Bryan men simply didn't have much luck when it came to marriage. Maybe he'd just been carrying on the family tradition. His mouth twisted in a humorless smile. The third generation of marriages to end in divorce. At least this time there hadn't been any children involved, he thought, remembering his parents' stormy union and eventual parting.

One thing his brief marriage had taught him was not to mistake lust for love. He'd wanted Roxanne enough to convince himself that the ache in his groin was caused by an equally strong ache in his heart. It wasn't a mistake he planned to make again. Which was why the decision to hire or fire Megan Roarke was not as easy as it might have been.

He'd wanted Roxanne, and look where that had gotten him. His desire for Megan was, if anything, even stronger than what he'd felt for his ex-wife. But he wasn't twenty-five anymore—full of ideals and still thinking he could succeed where his father and his grandfather had both failed. He was thirty-six, and well beyond the stage of thinking with his zipper.

There was a tapping at the door, and Kel was immediately aware of a subtle pressure behind that same zipper. He ground his teeth together, forcing back his automatic response. It was getting pretty bad when she didn't even have to be in the room to elicit this response.

"Come in," he snapped.

He didn't sound particularly welcoming. Megan swallowed hard and pushed open the door. Bearding the lion in his den, she thought, wishing it didn't seem quite such an accurate description.

She'd known this talk was coming. But she didn't have any idea what he was going to say. She didn't believe that he could have any complaints about how well she'd done her job. Certainly, Colleen had none.

But there was that odd tension that lay between her and Kel, that awareness that made her skin tingle whenever he walked in the room. She knew he felt it, too. Knew, also, that he didn't like it. He might just decide that it would be easier to let her go.

Kel was standing in front of his desk when Megan entered and she hesitated a moment just inside the door, struck, as always, by the impact he had on her senses. She would have thought that, after a week, the effect would have lessened somewhat, but it hadn't. She still felt a little weak-kneed and breathless every time she saw him.

"Have a seat," he said, gesturing to a comfortable-looking leather chair.

Megan shook her head and came farther into the room. "I think I'd rather stand."

"You look like you're facing a firing squad." He lifted one dark brow as his eyes raked over her tense expression.

"Should I ask for a blindfold?" she asked.

"I don't think so."

Kel leaned back against the desk, bracing his hands on either side of his hips and angling his long legs out in front of him.

"You've done a good job," he said, apparently deciding to cut through the preliminaries and right to the heart of the matter. "But then, you know that."

It wasn't exactly a question, but Megan chose to answer him anyway. "I told you I'd be good at this job," she said evenly.

"Well, you are." He paused and ran his fingers through his hair, looking uncharacteristically undecided. "Very good," he added, half to himself.

"Thank you." *He isn't going to offer me the job,* she thought. *He's decided that the sexual awareness between us offers too much potential for trouble, and he's going to tell me thanks but no thanks.*

"I'd like you to stay on," Kel said slowly, as if the words were pulled from him. "But there are a couple of things we need to discuss," he added, before she could decide whether the surge of emotion she felt was relief or panic.

"What kind of things?"

"First of all, the job is only going to last two or three months."

"I know that."

"Once her daughter has her baby and gets back on her feet, Gracie will be coming back."

"You said up front that it was only a temporary job," Megan said, nodding her understanding. "That suits me."

"So you said. I just wanted to be sure we were clear on that." He straightened away from the desk, and Megan had to suppress the urge to step back so that he wouldn't seem to loom over her.

"I understand that it's a temporary job," she said again, as much to prevent the silence from stretching as anything else.

"Good." He ran his hand through his hair again, rumpling it into thick, dark waves, and she had to curl her fingers into her palms against the desire to smooth it back into place.

"What else?"

"What else?" He looked at her, his eyes brooding and shadowed.

"You said there were a couple of things we needed to discuss," she reminded him.

"Right."

But he didn't say anything, only continued to watch her, those green eyes seeming to see right through to her soul. Her pulse, never completely steady when he was around, began to beat too quickly, making her feel breathless. Or maybe it was just being so close to him that made her breathless. And wasn't he closer than he had been a moment ago?

"What was it you wanted to discuss?" She could barely get the words out past the tightness in her throat.

"Just this."

His big hand cupped the back of her neck, tilting her head. Suddenly there was not even a heartbeat of space between them. And then his mouth came down on hers and Megan forgot all about breathing.

There was nothing tentative about the kiss, none of the gentle exploration that normally went with a first kiss. For an instant, Megan stood paralyzed in his embrace, feeling the impact of his mouth on hers all the way to her toes.

And then her arms went around his neck and she was rising on tiptoe to get closer to him, to deepen the kiss. She felt the brush of his mustache against her upper lip, soft in comparison to the firmness of his mouth. He always showered before dinner, and he smelled of soap and masculinity, a tantalizing combination that made her want to get closer still, until not even a shadow could find its way between them.

This was what she'd wanted since they'd met, what they'd both wanted. Giving in to the urge that had haunted her all week, Megan let her hand slide upward, her fingers slipping into the thick darkness of his hair. She felt as if she'd waited her entire life for this kiss, this moment. This man.

She tasted every bit as sweet as he'd imagined, Kel thought, half in despair. He'd almost managed to convince himself that one taste would be all he'd need. Once he'd kissed her, satisfied the sexual curiosity that had plagued him since she'd walked into the restaurant in Casper, he'd be satisfied. The tension would be broken and he would no longer be contemplating cold showers in the middle of the night. He'd almost believed it.

And then she'd melted into his arms, her slender body fitting itself to his as if made to be there. He could feel the fullness of her breasts against the muscled wall of his chest, and the softness of her belly cushioned the hardness of his arousal. And he knew one kiss would never be enough. A kiss would only serve to whet his appetite, a teasing taste of what could be.

He groaned against her mouth and widened his stance, drawing her forward so that she was cradled against his aching arousal. He groaned again when he felt the shiver that went through her. God, she was every bit as responsive as he'd dreamed.

His tongue traced the seam of her lips and she opened to him immediately. Kel wondered if he'd died and gone to heaven, because it didn't seem possible that anything this side of the pearly gates could taste as sweet as the damp softness of her tongue against his. On the other hand, what he was feeling now was way too carnal to have anything to do with heaven.

There was a big leather sofa only a few short steps away, a sly voice whispered in his ear. The thought of easing her down on it, feeling her slim body sink into the smooth black leather as he followed her down had his pulse drumming in his temples. The desk was even closer, he thought as he flattened his palm against her back. A sweep of his arm would clear its surface in an instant.

Megan's fingers curled into the thick darkness of Kel's hair as the world spun around her. The thrust of his tongue in her mouth, the feel of his big body against hers—those were the only things that were real to her at the moment.

She'd been kissed before but it had never been like this. She'd never had this feeling of losing herself in a man's touch, of giving up control of herself to him. If he chose to lay her on the floor and take her right then and there, she wasn't sure she would have lifted a finger in protest.

When she felt Kel begin to break off the kiss, she couldn't prevent a small whimper of protest, her lips clinging to his for a moment. She was reluctant to let him go, to let reality return.

Her fingers slipped from his hair as he eased her down until she felt the floor under her heels again. Kel's hands lingered on her for a moment longer, steadying her, before being withdrawn, leaving her standing on her own.

Her eyelids felt weighted and it took a conscious effort to lift them. His face was all hard planes and angles in the lamplight. The blatant hunger in his emerald eyes did nothing to put strength into her knees. Her gaze dropped to his mouth, but that was no better. She could still feel the gentle abrasion of his mustache against her skin, the warm heat of his mouth on hers.

He was so close. She only had to lean forward for them to be touching. The thought made her feel dizzy. What was happening to her? What had almost happened here? If he hadn't drawn back, would she have gathered her senses in time to stop what was happening? Would she even have wanted to? And how on earth was she supposed to think with him so close?

As if reading her thoughts, Kel stepped back a pace. Megan felt relief but she also felt bereft. She wanted to turn and run and she wanted to feel his arms around her again, his mouth driving out all rational thought.

"I just thought we should get that out in the open," Kel said, his voice husky and disturbed. "If you take this job, we might as well admit what's going to happen."

"What's going to happen?" Her voice was unsteady, but considering she felt on the verge of melting in a puddle at his feet, she wasn't going to complain about that.

"We're going to become lovers."

"Oh." It came out on a sharp exhale.

Lovers. The word started a warm throbbing feeling in the pit of her stomach. Kel Bryan would be her lover.

"Is sleeping with you part of the job description?" she asked, proud of the steadiness of her voice.

"Would you stay if it was?" He stroked the tips of his fingers down her cheek and she felt her pulse flutter in response.

"No," she managed to get out. But she admitted privately that the idea wasn't as offensive as it should have been.

"It's not a requirement." He withdrew his hand and she dragged a steadying breath into her lungs. "But it's going to happen, Megan. We both know it is."

Yes. She wouldn't lie to herself and pretend that it wasn't going to happen. For a moment, she resented him for bringing it out into the open, for making it impossible to pretend.

"Do you still want the job?" he asked.

Are we going to be lovers? he meant.

She stared at him, feeling her heart thumping against her rib cage, her skin still tingling from his touch. She should run, she thought. Before she ended up with a broken heart. Before Kel Bryan wound himself any more deeply into her life.

"I'll stay," she said.

"Good." Just one word but it held a wealth of satisfaction. He held out his hand and Megan responded automatically, putting her fingers in his. The familiar tingle was there, along with a new, much deeper awareness. Her eyes widened and she gave him a startled look as his fingers tightened around hers, drawing her toward him.

"All the best agreements are sealed with a kiss," he murmured, just before his mouth closed over hers.

Megan could only agree.

Chapter 5

Megan stumbled from Kel's study and sought the sanctuary of her room. Colleen was probably waiting to hear the results of her interview but Megan wasn't up to talking to her. She wasn't sure there was even enough strength left in her knees to get up the stairs as it was. She shut the bedroom door and leaned against it with her eyes closed.

She'd just agreed to have an affair with Kel Bryan.

The thought made her skin heat, and her pulse, none too steady to start with, fluttered in her throat. She might not have said the words but there was no doubt about what she'd agreed to do.

We're going to become lovers, he'd said and she hadn't argued. How could she when she knew it was nothing more than the truth? She was going to become Kel Bryan's lover. The thought was enough to make her dizzy. Or maybe it was the memory of his kisses that did that.

With an effort, Megan pushed herself away from the door and walked across the room to the connecting bathroom. Her knees were finally starting to feel a bit less like overcooked spaghetti. Flipping on the light, she set her palms on the edge of the sink and leaned forward to stare in the mirror.

She hardly recognized her own reflection. There was a sparkle in her eyes she'd never seen before, and her cheeks were flushed. Her softly swollen mouth left no doubt that she'd just been thoroughly kissed, and the smile that curved her lips made it obvious that she'd enjoyed it very much.

Kel Bryan's lover.

Her smile widened. She liked the sound of that more than she had any business doing.

Megan slept later than usual the morning after her interview with Kel, and when she got downstairs, the kitchen was empty, a fresh pot of coffee the only sign that Kel had been there at all. She was both disappointed and relieved.

Since she didn't know what to expect from him when she saw him again she was not averse to delaying the moment a while longer. Maybe by then, she'd have gotten her unruly reaction under control.

As it happened, she didn't see Kel until he came in for dinner. She was sliding a pan of biscuits into the oven when she heard the kitchen door open. She didn't have to turn around to know who it was. Even if she hadn't heard the door open, she would have known he was in the room. She could feel it in the sudden sensitivity of her skin.

Willing her hand to steadiness, she set down the pot holder she'd been using and turned toward him. He stood just inside the door—big, dusty, overwhelmingly male. Her heart thumped and it occurred to her vaguely that there was a warning there. It was one thing to decide to have an affair with the man, something else altogether for just the sight of him to make her heart beat faster.

He set his hat on the wooden hook beside the door and turned toward her. Their eyes met and Megan thought she saw a quick flare of awareness in his. Was he remembering the way she'd melted against him last night? The memory made her flush, and she hoped he'd attribute it to the fact that she'd just been leaning over a hot oven.

His eyes raked over her, taking in the robin's egg blue T-shirt and jeans she wore, a practical white chef's apron wrapped around her waist. Not exactly a romantic outfit in which to greet your future lover, Megan thought. And she probably had flour on her face from making the biscuits. A touch of humor glimmered in her eyes. Kel was probably wondering what had made him want to kiss her the night before.

Actually, Kel was on the point of closing the distance between them, dragging Megan into his arms and kissing her senseless, flour-speckled face and all. If Colleen hadn't chosen that moment to enter the kitchen, he might have done just that.

With a quick greeting for his sister and an impersonal nod in Megan's direction, he went upstairs to shower before dinner. By the time he came down, he had himself well under control. Or so he thought until he walked into the dining room and saw Megan leaning across the table to straighten a fork on the side across from her. The scoop neckline of her T-shirt allowed him to see the upper swell of her breasts and hinted at the shadowy cleft between.

Kel immediately wished he'd taken a colder shower than he had.

He backed out of the room without her seeing him and didn't enter until he heard Gun's voice and knew he wouldn't be alone with Megan. The way he was feeling right now, he didn't quite trust himself not to give in to the urge to ignore the delicious scents wafting from the kitchen and have *her* for dinner instead of whatever she was cooking.

Kel avoided looking at Megan any more than he had to during dinner. He was starting to resent this strange hold she seemed to have over him. He'd spent far more time thinking about her today than he'd had any business doing. He didn't like the way she haunted his thoughts.

He was a man who prided himself on his self-control, and he resented Megan Roarke's ability to undermine that control. He wanted her—that much he was willing to admit. Hell, he could hardly deny it. Wanting her was all right but letting her dominate his thoughts the way she had been—that was going to have to stop.

If he could stop it.

The taunting voice inside his head only made Kel more determined to prove to himself that *he* was in control here, not his suddenly overactive libido. And if that meant keeping his distance from Megan, then so be it.

By the end of her second week working on the Lazy B, Megan was starting to wonder if she'd hallucinated the scene in Kel's study the night he'd asked her to stay on for the summer. She hadn't been quite sure what to expect after the passionate kisses they'd shared but it certainly wasn't that everything would go on just as it had before he kissed her.

She hadn't expected him to pounce—not exactly anyway. And she didn't want to bring their relationship—if and when they had one—out into the open any more than he did. She wasn't sure how Colleen would feel about Megan sleeping with her older brother, but Megan knew it would embarrass her if Colleen were to find out about it. She supposed there were women sophisticated enough to carry off something like that, but she wasn't one of them.

So at first, she'd been grateful for Kel's discretion. But as the days ticked by and he made no effort to seek out even a brief moment of privacy with her, she began to question her memory. She was grateful that he wasn't trying to rush her, but a stolen kiss or two wouldn't be out of line.

But Kel didn't seem to have any interest in kisses—stolen or otherwise. He treated her just as he had before, friendly but a little distant. The perfect employer-to-employee attitude, she thought with some irritation. She might have believed she'd imagined the entire exchange between them if it hadn't been for the one or two occasions she caught him looking at her and saw that the indifference was gone, replaced by a blazing green heat that burned right through her.

He still wanted her but, for reasons of his own, he was keeping his distance. Megan would have given a great deal to know what those reasons were but she could hardly come right out and ask the man why he hadn't tried to seduce her. Not that he was likely to have to try too hard, she admitted, remembering the way he'd melted her defenses with a touch.

Still, if he expected her to make the first move, Kel Bryan had another think coming.

So Megan's apparent indifference mirrored Kel's own.

He resented the hell out of her casual attitude.

She resented the hell out of his.

And the sexual tension smoldered—unacknowl-edged—between them.

It was left to Colleen to unwittingly end the stale-mate created by stubborn pride. Sunday was as close to a day of rest as was possible on a working ranch. There were always chores to be done but on Sunday they were limited to the most basic—such as animals to be cared for—or the least taxing—such as tack to be cleaned or repaired.

Megan suspected that the tradition had its origins less in religion than in necessity since quite a few of the hands made it a point to drive into the nearest town on Saturday night and put as much effort into having a good time as they put into their work the rest of the week. The result was a bunch of grown men walking very carefully Sunday morning, as if not entirely sure their heads were going to stay in place.

Technically, Megan had Sunday off, as well as one other day a week of her own choosing. Since the nearest town consisted of three bars, two gas stations and a general store that housed an eclectic mix of merchandise, it hardly seemed worth the effort to go there. The two Sundays she'd spent on the Lazy B, Megan had used the time to clean up odds and ends of jobs she hadn't quite managed to finish and to do fancier baking than she took time for during the week.

One thing about cooking for men who spent ten hours a day doing hard, physical labor was that they seemed to burn an amazing number of calories. And nobody seemed to worry much about things like cholesterol, which meant she could indulge her love of baking and not feel so much as a twinge of guilt.

But on this Sunday, Colleen announced that Megan was not to lift a finger. "You've done nothing but work since you came here," she said.

"That's what I was hired to do," Megan pointed out.

"You weren't hired to be slave labor. You haven't taken a single day off."

"I don't feel overworked."

"Everyone needs time off," Colleen insisted. "Shouldn't Megan take today off?" She looked across the room at her brother, who'd just entered. Megan immediately became terribly interested in the crossword puzzle she'd been toying with.

"I thought today *was* her day off." Megan felt Kel's eyes on her but she didn't look up.

"It is, but if she stays here, she'll end up working. You know she will."

Kel hadn't paid enough attention to her to have any idea what she did with her time, Megan thought irritably. She didn't have to lift her eyes from the paper to know that he was still looking at her.

"Can you ride?"

The question had to have been addressed to her but it took Megan a moment to gather her wits enough to respond. She looked at him, feeling her breath catch a little, just as it always did when their eyes met.

"It's been a few years," she said cautiously.

"She could ride Mickey," Colleen suggested enthusiastically. "He's gentle enough for a baby."

"Mickey?" Megan asked.

"As in Mouse." Kel's tone was dry. "Colleen named him," he added with a mock-disgusted look in his sister's direction.

"I was eight," she said defensively. "Besides, he's as gentle as a mouse so it's a good name for him."

"It was the last time Dad or I let her name a horse," Kel told Megan.

"So there's no Minnie?" For the first time in over a week, she felt at ease with him.

"No. But if we hadn't stopped her, I suspect we'd have had a full complement of horses named after cartoon characters."

"Imagine a stallion named Donald Duck." Megan shook her head sympathetically at Kel's exaggerated shudder.

"Laugh all you want," Colleen said, giving them both an offended look. "But I still think Mickey is the perfect horse for Megan."

Which was how Megan found herself riding away from the ranch house on a bay gelding named Mickey Mouse. Kel was beside her on the big black horse she'd seen him riding that first day. The black's name was Dude, which she assumed referred to his somewhat flashy beauty.

They made a striking pair, she thought, stealing a sideways glance at Kel and the big horse. Two superbly healthy male animals, in the prime of life, arrogantly confident of their place in the world. Kel rode as if he was a part of the horse, his body hardly seeming to move in the saddle. In contrast, Megan felt as if she was bouncing up and down like a loosely filled sack of potatoes.

"Loosen up," Kel said, apparently reading her thoughts. "Slouch down in the saddle a little and let yourself feel the rhythm of the horse."

She did her best to do as he'd instructed and it did seem to help a little. But she still envied him the utter ease with which he sat a horse. In his faded jeans and one of the chambray shirts that seemed to compose a large part of his wardrobe, the gray hat pulled low over his eyes, his hands and knees easily controlling the big horse, he looked as if he'd stepped out of a painting of the old West. All he needed was a duster tied to the back of the saddle and a rifle in its scabbard, maybe a pair of revolvers tied low.

Megan caught his questioning glance and looked away, embarrassed at having been caught fantasizing, even if he couldn't possibly know what she'd been thinking. She forced herself to concentrate on the view between Mickey's ears. There was plenty to see. Spread out before them was a sweep of land and sky so vast it was almost impossible to take in.

She'd spent all her time since coming to work for Kel either in or near the ranch house, which nestled in the shoulder of low hills that served to soften the view a little. She'd almost forgotten the sheer emptiness of the landscape that surrounded it.

She turned in the saddle to look back. The ranch house was no longer visible. In all that vast expanse of land, there were only the two of them. It had never occurred to her that so much space could be oppressive. Yet it was also exhilarating.

Kel watched Megan, trying to judge her reaction. Not everyone appreciated wide-open sky and empty plains. He'd taken Roxanne out riding not long after they were married. She'd hated every moment of the experience, starting with the Western-style saddle and ending with the barrenness of the land. It made her feel small, she'd complained, hunching her shoulders as if for protection against the emptiness of the land and sky.

Looking back, Kel supposed he should have known then that the marriage was a mistake, but when he took her to the ranch house, she'd coaxed him up to their bedroom and provided a vivid reminder of their one area of compatibility.

He saw Megan turn in the saddle to look in the direction they'd come. He knew the ranch house was out of sight and that it seemed as if they'd left all signs of civilization behind. She glanced up at the blue arc of sky and hunched her shoulders uneasily. Kel's fingers tightened on Dude's reins in anticipation of Megan's request to turn back.

But after a moment, she straightened her shoulders and he saw her breasts lift as she took a deep breath. She released it slowly and then glanced at him.

"I've read about pioneers who went mad because they couldn't deal with the emptiness of the prairie," she said slowly. "For the first time, I think I can understand how they must have felt."

"It can be a bit overwhelming," Kel agreed. He was still prepared to turn around.

"Yes. But it's magnificent, too. And so quiet." She sighed, her eyes going a little dreamy. "I can see why the Indians fought so hard to keep their land. If I had a place like this, I wouldn't want to let it go."

Kel relaxed his hand on the reins and smiled at her, feeling something strangely like pride uncurl inside him. Not that he had any business being proud of Megan Roarke, he reminded himself. Whether she liked the wide-open Wyoming sky or not was a matter of interest but not real concern. Not like it had been with Roxanne. He'd been married to Roxanne and it had mattered that she'd been unable to see the beauty in the land around her.

He wanted Megan as his lover, not his wife, and even if she'd hated the ranch, it wouldn't have mattered. Still, that vague feeling of pride didn't go away.

* * *

They talked easily. Megan had been reading up on Wyoming's history and was fascinated to know that they were right in the middle of Johnson County, site of the notorious Johnson County War. When she heard that his great-grandfather had actually known Nate Champion, who'd posthumously become something of a hero after the war, Megan's excitement lit up her eyes. Her fascination with the man made Kel glad Champion had been dead for a good hundred years. He thought, ruefully, that he wasn't sure he could have stood up to the competition.

Since Megan had little experience as a rider, Kel had no intention of taking her very far from the ranch house on this first trip. Even a short ride was going to leave her stiff and sore. Of course, if he'd been sure she'd be willing to let him massage the ache from her muscles, he might have been tempted to make it a longer trip.

"We'll stop at the creek," he said, nodding to the band of trees they were approaching. "It's a good place for a picnic. There's plenty of shade."

"I guess that's something of a rarity around here, isn't it?"

"Trees aren't real plentiful," he agreed. "Not until you get into the foothills."

Though Colleen had loaned her a hat to shield her from the hot summer sun, Megan sighed with relief as they rode into the trees that lined the edge of the creek. It wasn't the kind of woods she'd known in Minnesota, really not much more than a ragged scattering of cottonwoods and shrubs taking advantage of a reliable source of water in a place where such things were not common. But it was a pleasant swath of green amidst the dun-colored land that surrounded it.

Kel swung out of the saddle and looped Dude's reins over a low branch on one of the shrubs. "Here. Let me help you down," he said, glancing over his shoulder to where she sat perched on Mickey's broad back.

"It looks a lot farther than I'd realized," she admitted as she swung her leg over the saddle and leaned down to put her hands on his broad shoulders.

She'd been so busy worrying about how she was going to get off the horse that she was caught off guard by the familiar jolt of electricity that arced between them, even at that casual touch. Her eyes jerked to Kel's as she felt his hands close around her waist. Any doubts she might have had about whether or not he still wanted her vanished beneath the heated green of his gaze.

It had been a mistake to touch her, Kel thought. The last two and a half weeks had been sheer torture. And the brief taste of her in his office had only added to the torture. And damned if his fingers didn't nearly span her waist, just the way he'd imagined they would.

He lifted her from the saddle and Megan's hands shifted to grab the muscles in his upper arms. They were like iron beneath her fingers, and the easy way he held her made her vividly aware of the difference in strength between them. He took his time about lowering her to the ground, drawing her forward so that she slid slowly—so very slowly—down the length of his body. And all the while, he held her gaze with his, those clear green eyes dark with hunger. A hunger that found an echo in the pit of her stomach.

She could hear the soft babble of the creek behind her and somewhere high overhead was the wild cry of a hawk as it painted lazy circles in the clear blue sky. A tiny breeze rustled the leaves on the cottonwoods, a breath of air on the hot stillness of a summer's day.

But Megan was oblivious to everything but the ragged pounding of her own heart. And the heat in Kel Bryan's look.

She felt the hard, metallic pressure of his belt buckle against her belly and then he lowered her a few more inches and she felt the stir of his arousal through the denim of his jeans. Her breath caught in an audible gasp and her fingers flexed against his arms, like a cat kneading her paws.

She felt the ground beneath her toes and then felt it knocked out from under her again as Kel's mouth came down on hers.

There was nothing gentle about the kiss. Just like before, there was no tentative exploration, no coaxing a response. There was no need for it. Megan's mouth opened to his like a drought-stricken flower opening to life-giving rain. She shivered as his tongue thrust deep inside, claiming her in a fundamental way.

He smelled of shaving soap, sun and a faintly earthy smell that she could only label rugged male. His mouth found the pulse that beat just under her ear, tasting it with his tongue before his teeth nipped at her earlobe, sending soft shivers down her spine.

She felt a tug against her scalp as he pulled loose the elastic band that held her hair at the base of her neck.

His fingers speared deep into the silken mass, his big hand cupping the back of her head, tilting her face toward his as his mouth descended on hers again.

Her hands were not still. She flexed her fingers once more against the solid muscles of his arms, finding them about as yielding as a piece of well-cured oak. She knocked his hat from his head so that her fingers could delve into the thick darkness of his hair.

The world seemed to spin around her and it was only when Megan felt the ground come up beneath her back that she realized the sensation was not entirely the result of Kel's powerful effect on her senses. The buttons on her gray cotton shirt yielded to his impatient touch, and she gasped when she felt the heated weight of his hand flattened against her stomach.

He lifted his head to look down at her, his eyes holding her captive as his fingers slid upward. He opened the front clip on her bra with an easy expertise that Megan wasn't at all sure she liked. But then his hand closed over her breast and she liked that very much indeed.

Too much, she thought, even as his clever fingers drew a whimper of pleasure from her. It was too much. She was spinning out of control, giving herself over to him in a way that was half exhilarating, half frightening.

The fear won out. Not fear of Kel but fear of what he made her feel. She wasn't ready for this. Not yet. It was too much, too soon. He had only to touch her and she was on fire. Just the way it had been between them from the moment they'd met.

He was going to be her lover. She believed that, wanted it to happen. But not now, not when her head was spinning so that she hardly knew her own name. Megan opened her mouth to tell him that she wanted to stop.

His head dipped and her breath left her in a startled moan as she felt the moist heat of his tongue against her nipple. Streaks of lightning seemed to run from that tiny point all the way down to her toes, melting bone and muscle on the way. Her hands came up, her fingers threading through his hair.

Push him away, she told herself.

Draw him closer.

Need shuddered through her as he took her into his mouth, licking and sucking, doing things she'd only read about until now and had never really imagined actually happening to her. His mustache brushed against her skin, its gentle abrasion a contrast to the moist heat of his mouth.

It had to stop now.

I'd die if it ever stopped.

His hair curled over her fingers like dark silk. She swallowed a whimper of pleasure. It would be so easy to give in, to let him make love to her in the soft green grass, sheltered by the cottonwoods, with only the pale blue Wyoming sky for a witness. She wanted him.

But she wasn't ready for this. Not yet.

"Kel." It was as much a whimper as a word. His fingers had closed over her other breast, teasing the nipple to swollen attention. She was drowning in sensation. But everything was moving too quickly. It was too much, too soon. They'd barely spoken this past week, now they were on the verge of making love. She needed more time.

"No."

There was no force behind the word. In fact, she was half surprised she'd even managed to get it out. But she knew Kel heard it, could feel the sudden stillness of his body against hers.

For the space of several heartbeats, he didn't move. She could feel the roughness of his cheek against the tender skin of her breast, the firm pressure of his arousal against her hip. Somewhere in the back of her mind, it occurred to Megan that there was nothing to stop him from forcing the issue.

Not that he'd have to use force, she admitted honestly. He had to know that it wouldn't take much persuasion to change her mind. There was even a small part of her that hoped he would ignore her protest, that he'd kiss her into silence and satisfy the hunger that rolled in long, trembling waves through her body.

It wouldn't take much to get her to change her mind. The thought rolled through Kel's mind. She was quivering under his touch, a heartbeat away from giving him what he wanted—what they both wanted. He could make her forget her doubts, make her forget everything but how good they were together.

Megan saw the effort it cost Kel to lift his head and let his hand slide from her. Immediately, she felt bereft and more than half wished she'd ignored the voice of reason. It was especially difficult to hold onto her crumbling sanity when she met the searing heat in his eyes.

"I'm not ready for this," she said, flushing a little as the throbbing ache in the pit of her stomach called her a liar.

"All right." Kel's voice was huskier than usual.

Megan was vividly aware of the hard ridge of arousal still pressed against her hip. A wave of purely feminine guilt washed over her, and she could hear her grandmother warning her of the terrible things that befell girls who teased.

"I'm sorry. I should have called a halt sooner."

"I don't recall giving you much chance to say anything."

She jumped as his hand flattened over her belly. Her skin was so sensitive that she could feel the imprint of each finger separate from the others.

"But I should have said something sooner. I shouldn't have let..." She trailed off as she saw the unmistakable glint of humor in his eyes. The last thing she'd expected was for him to see any humor in the situation, and she was torn between relief and annoyance.

"Are you apologizing because you think I'm now in mortal agony?" he asked her.

"I know it's painful for a man..." she began primly.

"That's an old wive's tale, honey. It was invented by teenage boys to convince teenage girls that they really *want* to lose their cherry in the back of a Chevy."

Megan's face flushed at his blunt summation but she swallowed hard and refused to look away. "Aren't you...I mean, doesn't it..."

"I'll admit I've been more comfortable in my day," he admitted. *God, that was the understatement of the year.* He ached so much it seemed as if even his hair hurt. "I'm not any more uncomfortable than you are," he continued, shifting his hand against the taut skin of her stomach, feeling the quiver of her response. "Men just aren't built to hide our reactions the way women can."

Megan felt herself flush again but she couldn't deny that her body wasn't particularly happy about the interruption her mind had insisted was necessary.

"You don't mind?"

"Oh, I mind. But I'll survive." His laugh held a tinge of pain, and Megan found herself oddly pleased by the sound. There was no logic to it but she didn't like the idea that he could end what had been happening without feeling at least a twinge of discomfort.

She gasped when she felt the brush of his fingertip across the still taut peak of her breast. Echoes of that touch rippled through her, bringing her nerve endings to quivering life.

"Kel..."

"I'm not going to try to get you to change your mind," he said. "But there's no harm in a little petting, is there?"

"Petting? You mean like teenagers at a drive-in?" She eyed him warily.

"It's allowed even when you're over sixteen," he said, his mouth quirking with humor.

"I don't think—"

He stopped her uncertain protest with a kiss, and when he lifted his head, she'd forgotten what she'd been saying.

"Don't think. I won't do anything you don't want."

Yes, but what about things I do want but shouldn't,
Megan wondered despairingly as the callused roughness of his thumb stroked across her swollen nipple.

"We won't take off any clothes. We'll just spend
some time getting to know each other." He nibbled the
soft skin along her jaw and Megan shivered.

She'd always thought of getting to know each other
as being a more cerebral activity. Maybe they'd talk
about books they liked or their childhoods or the state
of world affairs. Kel's tongue tasted the pulse that beat
much too quickly at the base of her throat. She arched
her neck in unconscious invitation. Of course, she
supposed there was knowing and then there was
knowing. Kel's version certainly had its advantages.

"Just pretend you're sweet sixteen and that we're in
my Daddy's fifty-six Chevy." He kissed his way along
the fragile ridge of her collarbone. "We're parked at
the end of a long, lonely road with nothing but the
stars for company. Unbutton my shirt."

"This is crazy." But her trembling fingers were already working the buttons of his shirt. "It's broad
daylight."

"Shh." He took her mouth in a quick biting kiss,
sweet punishment for being too practical. "It's after
eleven and I promised your father I'd have you home
by midnight. We've only got a little while and we have
to make the most of it."

Megan curled her fingers into the mat of dark, curly
hair that covered his chest, feeling herself falling into
the fantasy he was creating. He caught her hands in
his, pinning them to the soft green grass on either side
of her head as he lowered his body over hers.

Kel wasn't sure why he was torturing himself like this. He should roll away from her, get up, get on his horse and put some distance between them. On second thoughts, riding a horse wasn't such a good idea at the moment. And she smelled so good. And she tasted even better.

"Hear the crickets outside the car?" he whispered against her ear.

Megan couldn't hear anything above the thunderous rhythm of her heartbeat. The hard muscles of his chest pressed against her breasts, the crisp mat of hair abrading their already sensitized peaks.

She opened her eyes and stared at him. "I...I've never necked in a parked car in my life," she whispered, not sure if it was a protest or merely a comment.

"Let me show you what you missed," he said. His mustache lifted in a wicked grin that made her curl her toes inside her shoes.

"This is crazy," she whispered but her mouth opened to his, and for a moment, she almost believed she could hear those stupid crickets.

Chapter 6

"I'm going to have to rebuild the engine," Gun said, staring into the engine compartment.

"I think a small nuclear bomb would be a better idea." Megan shook her head when she saw the condition of the engine. "I hope you didn't pay much for this thing because if it cost you more than a buck and a quarter, you got rooked."

"This car is worth a fortune," Gun protested, giving the battered Corvette a proud look. "It's got a four fifty-four with four hundred and sixty horsepower. It's the biggest engine they made."

"It's not much more than a pile of rubble," Megan said. She put her hand through a hole in the fiberglass fender to demonstrate.

"It's got the original engine," he said stubbornly. "That's important."

"It needs about a thousand hours of work," she pointed out.

"You just don't know a diamond in the rough when you see one."

"It looks more like a cubic zirconia to me." But the laughter in her eyes took the sting out of the words.

"Just wait till I've got it put back together," Gun said, undeterred by her cynical attitude. "You'll eat those words."

"I'm willing to take that risk." It occurred to her that she'd be long gone by the time Gun finished restoring the Vette, but she shoved the thought away, just as she'd been doing with any thoughts that delved too far into the future.

"It's obvious that mechanic you worked for didn't appreciate a challenge," Gun said. He leaned into the engine compartment to poke at wires and cables.

"He taught me to recognize a hopeless case when I saw one," Megan countered.

She'd spent six months working for a mechanic in Seattle. Technically, she'd been hired as a secretary-receptionist but she'd ended up spending most of her time in the garage helping her employer. She'd learned a fair amount about the inner workings of a car and might have stayed longer if the man's nephew hadn't been laid off. Since his nephew had two children to support, Bill had felt obliged to offer him a job—*her* job. *Family's got to take care of each other,* Bill had told her regretfully. She'd heard her grandfather say much the same, though he'd usually managed to get the word *duty* in. And he'd generally been looking at his only grandchild when he said it, his mouth drawn tight, making it clear that duty could be quite painful.

"It's not as bad as it looks," Gun said, drawing Megan's attention back to the present. "Once the engine is rebuilt, I'll find someone to do the bodywork."

"There's not enough body left to work on."

"Did anyone ever tell you that you have a negative attitude?" He shook his head sadly but there was laughter in those incredible blue eyes of his.

"Realistic." Megan grinned at him.

She'd come to like Gun in the three weeks she'd worked on the Lazy B. It was hard to imagine *not* liking Gun. Considering his rather remarkable good looks, it wouldn't have been surprising if he'd turned out to be a conceited jerk. But if he was aware of his attractiveness—and how could he not be?—she'd never seen any sign of it.

He was rarely without a smile, but she sometimes wondered if the charm he wielded so easily was as much a shield as anything else. Could the subtle tension that lay between him and Colleen have anything to do with the sadness she thought she sensed in Gun?

"If you talk to me real nice, I might let you help me pull the engine," Gun said with the air of one proffering a rare treat.

"Be still, my heart." Megan rolled her eyes in a fair semblance of someone on the verge of fainting from excitement.

"Careful with the sarcasm or I'll have to find myself another mechanic's assistant," he warned mockingly.

Sunlight caught in Gun's hair as he leaned forward, drawing her attention to the spark-plug wires, which looked as if they'd been installed about the time the *Titanic* was setting sail. He really was gorgeous, she thought, studying his profile. On a purely objective level, he was probably even better looking than Kel.

But there was nothing objective about her feelings for Kel. Just being in the same room with him made her heart beat faster. It had been like that from the moment they'd met. And the effect had done nothing but grow stronger.

Especially this past week. Megan felt her cheeks warm at the memory of their ride to the creek. She didn't know if she'd improved her skills as a rider but she'd certainly learned a thing or two about herself as a woman.

"Do you always blush at the sight of a corroded spark plug?" Gun's teasing question snapped Megan out of her thoughts.

She blinked and focused her eyes on him. "The sight of corrosion makes my blood pressure rise," she said lightly.

"And I thought it might be the look Kel's giving you that brought the color to your cheeks."

"Kel?" Megan's head jerked in the direction Gun had nodded.

Kel was just coming out of the barn leading Dude. Distance and the hat he wore made it impossible to tell if he was looking at her but Megan knew he was. She could feel his eyes on her, as tangible as a touch. She smiled, wondering if he'd come over to say hello.

Not that he hadn't said a very thorough hello at breakfast this morning. The memory made her flush. She'd half expected him to go back to treating her the way he had before their ride. But whatever it was that had made him keep his distance, he'd apparently changed his mind. In the week since then, they'd exchanged several kisses hot enough to steam paint off any walls they might happen to be standing near.

Kel swung himself into the saddle, and Megan had to swallow a sigh. As always, the sight of him on the big black horse made her think of cigarette commercials and wide beds, not necessarily in that order.

She thought he hesitated a moment, as if thinking about walking Dude over to where she and Gun stood next to the Corvette. But if so, he must have changed his mind, because he merely touched his hand to the brim of his hat in a classic Western gesture and reined Dude's head around. Megan watched until the shoulder of one of the surrounding hills blocked him from sight.

Kel frowned at the view between Dude's ears. He didn't like the way he'd felt when he saw Megan with Gun. He didn't like it because it felt suspiciously like jealousy and he didn't want to care enough to be jealous. Hell, he hadn't even been jealous of Roxanne and he'd been married to her. Of course, by the time he'd figured out that there was cause for jealousy, their marriage had been too far gone for him to feel much beyond disgust.

Not that there was any cause for jealousy here. Even if he didn't trust Megan, he trusted Gun. They'd been friends all their lives. Gun could charm a bear away from honey but he'd never betray a friend.

Of course, there was no way for Gun to know that anyone had a prior claim to Megan. Kel's frown deepened into a scowl. He hadn't talked to Megan about it but she didn't seem any more eager than he was to bring their relationship out in the open. He suspected she was enjoying the slightly wicked feeling of carrying on a secret intrigue.

And what's your excuse, Bryan?

He shifted uneasily in the saddle. He'd told himself that he didn't want to set a bad example for Colleen but it was a thin excuse at best. His little sister was no longer a child and the fact that her brother was a normal man with normal appetites wasn't likely to cause her any major trauma.

Maybe, like Megan, he was enjoying the secrecy. Once other people knew that they were lovers—which he sincerely hoped they were soon to be—then he'd have to deal with the sidelong glances, the speculation. And he'd be faced with the possibility of having to kill any of his men foolish enough to comment on Megan in his hearing.

But he wouldn't have to worry about anybody—say his good friend Gun, for instance—thinking that Megan was available. The image of Gun and Megan leaning over the engine compartment, their fair heads close together, lingered in Kel's memory.

He could trust Gun. But what about Megan? Nothing in his experience had given him reason to have much faith in women. He wasn't foolish enough to think that, because his mother had betrayed his father and Roxanne had, in her turn, betrayed him, it meant all women were not to be trusted. On the other hand, the track record of the Bryan men was such that he couldn't help but feel a little cautious.

Dude slowed and Kel, who hadn't been paying much attention to where he was, realized that they'd reached the stock tank he'd come out to check. It was a good thing his horse knew what he was supposed to be doing, Kel thought ruefully. He stepped out of the saddle and ground hitched the big horse by letting the reins drop to the dirt. There were a few head of cattle milling around the tank, and they cast a disinterested look in his direction as he approached.

Kel looked them over automatically, checking their condition. He was satisfied with what he saw. It had been a comparatively mild winter this year and a reasonably wet spring. The range was in good shape and so was the herd. If they didn't have a drought this summer or any of half a dozen other possible disasters, they'd do better than average this year.

Assured that the stock tank was clear and full, Kel swung into the saddle, but he didn't immediately nudge Dude into motion. He tilted his hat back and really looked at the land around him for the first time that day. From the time he was a boy, whenever he'd been upset or had suffered a disappointment, he'd always found solace in the land. He could remember riding out onto the range the day after his mother left for the final time. He'd known somehow that she wouldn't be back this time, not for him, not for Colleen, who'd been little more than an infant. It was the last time he could remember crying.

When Roxanne had departed for Boston, he'd helped her load her things in her car, watched her drive off, and then he'd saddled Dude and ridden for hours. He'd worked out his self-directed anger at having made such a stupid mistake, at having let his gonads do his thinking.

And here he was again. Except that this time was different. He couldn't really compare Megan to his mother or his ex-wife. She was only here for the summer. She wasn't a vital part of his life and he wasn't going to let that change. An affair—if she ever decided she was ready for one—would be nothing more than a summer diversion for both of them. The reminder made Kel feel better. She was temporary in his life. And he wouldn't want it any other way.

Feeling restless, Megan wandered out onto the porch. Colleen was occupied with her physical therapist, the house was clean, a batch of bread was rising on the kitchen counter. She wasn't in the mood for reading and it was too early to start preparations for dinner.

She wrapped her hands around one of the upright posts that supported the porch roof and stared moodily across the ranch yard. There were storm clouds to the north, hanging thick and heavy over the mountains. According to Kel, they'd probably have rain sometime tonight. She hadn't lived until she'd been through a summer lightning storm in Wyoming, Colleen had told her at breakfast.

Maybe she could blame the approaching storm for the fact that Colleen had gotten out of bed early this morning. This morning, of all mornings, when Megan had planned to talk to Kel, planned to tell him that... Tell him what? That she was having trouble sleeping nights because she lay awake thinking about him sleeping across the hall? That she was tired of this game of stealing kisses and quick caresses that left her aching? That she wanted him to make love to her?

It was the truth, but even if Colleen hadn't shown up for breakfast this morning, Megan wasn't sure she could have found the words to ask Kel Bryan to become her lover.

He'd told her that it would be up to her to let him know when she was ready to take the next step between them. After that incendiary encounter when he'd taken her riding, he'd promised not to push. The decision would be hers, he'd said, made without pressure.

He'd kept his word. She could hardly count kissing her as applying pressure, not when she'd been such an eager participant in those kisses. The fact that she'd spent the last two weeks in a state of tingling arousal wasn't entirely Kel's fault.

But it was definitely his fault that his self-control never faltered. Well, faltered, maybe, but never weakened to the point where he forgot all about his stupid promise to let her decide when they should take the next step.

Last night, for example, they'd been in his den, with the door shut and no one to bother them, and she'd been stretched out on the sofa with her blouse half off, Kel's big body—his very aroused body—pressed along the length of hers. There'd been nothing to stop him from taking her right then. Certainly, she wouldn't have whispered so much as a word of protest.

But he'd stopped, damn him. Even though he must have known she wasn't going to ask him to, he'd stopped. He'd pulled her to her feet and hooked her bra, buttoned her blouse, even stroked some semblance of order into her tangled hair. She'd stood there like a stick figure, feeling as if she'd just been spun by a hurricane, her thoughts tumbling one over the other in her head, moving too quickly for her to grab hold of any single one.

"You tell me when you're ready, Megan," he'd said, his voice raspy, his green eyes hungry.

She was ready. More than ready. She'd had plenty of time to think about it, to decide that this was what she wanted—to be Kel's lover, even if it was only for the summer.

But she hadn't been able to find the words to say as much. It was one thing to slide under the spell of passion he so effortlessly wove around her. It was something else altogether to stand there, flat-footed, and ask him to make love to her. But after a nearly sleepless night, she'd made up her mind that she was going to do exactly that. And Colleen had to choose this morning to get up early.

Megan sighed and released her hold on the post. Stepping off the porch, she bent to pluck a stalk of lamb's-quarter that had sprung up in the flower bed. She wandered down the path to the gate, plucking leaves off the plant as she went.

She considered herself a mature woman. She'd been traveling on her own since she was eighteen. She was accustomed to making her own decisions, taking responsibility for her own choices. In this case, it wasn't the decision that was hard to make. In a way, she'd made that particular choice when she'd come to work for Kel. It was just finding a way to tell him that was giving her fits.

Damn him for being such a gentleman, anyway.

Megan tossed aside the shredded lamb's-quarter and scowled at nothing in particular, her expression as gray as the clouds building to the north. She was about to turn back to the house when she noticed some of the ranch hands lined up along the rails of the fence that marked off the corral next to the barn. They seemed to be watching something inside the corral. Needing a distraction, Megan pushed open the gate and started across the packed dirt of the yard.

In the weeks since she'd come to work here, she'd gotten to know most of the men. The Lazy B was similar to the small town she'd first compared it to, and it wasn't possible to live in such a small community without becoming acquainted with its members.

An elderly and highly temperamental man by the name of Zeke did the cooking for the men, and Kel had warned her that Zeke was jealous of his status as cook. He'd started out on the Lazy B when Kel's grandfather owned the ranch, cowboying until he announced that his bones were too brittle for sitting a cayuse and that he'd take over the cooking, which until then had rotated among the men. His cooking was plain but filling, and the men had no complaints except when it came to baking. As one of the men had put it, if there was only a gun made to fire them,

Zeke's biscuits were hard enough to bring down a buffalo. Zeke had demonstrated the truth of this claim by throwing a panful at the cowboy in question. The resultant bruises had proved beyond a doubt that the biscuits were hard as rocks. Zeke thereafter refused to bake anything for a bunch of ingrates who ought to be thankful they'd found someone who'd hire their sorry asses, let alone feed 'em.

Megan had heard the story from Gun the first week she'd worked here. She'd asked what the cowboys did for bread, if Zeke refused to bake. Gun had told her that Zeke bought bread but he was ornery enough to buy the cheapest stuff he could find. Grace Cavenaugh had occasionally taken pity on the hands and made up a batch of biscuits or baked a couple of extra pies. Zeke allowed these intrusions on his territory only because Grace Cavenaugh had informed him that he was a no-good excuse for a human being and that if he opened his mouth to her, she'd take a frying pan to his mangy head.

Megan had laughed at the image and asked why Kel didn't do something about Zeke. Kel shook his head and grimaced. Zeke scared the hell out of him. The old coot had known him since he was in diapers and he wasn't at all impressed that Kel was now the boss. If Megan was smart, she'd keep her distance from Zeke.

Megan considered herself a smart woman but the challenge had simply been too much to resist. She'd waited until she was sure she was going to be staying on the ranch for the summer and then she'd made up a huge batch of feather rolls, using her grandmother's recipe. She'd carried them down to the bunkhouse and presented them to Zeke, who was every bit as crusty and intimidating as she'd been told. She wanted his recipe for venison stew, she'd announced, and she was willing to trade a batch of rolls for it.

Zeke had glared at her through a haze of cigarette smoke and told her to take her rolls and remove her fanny from his kitchen. Megan stood her ground. How did he think the cowboys were going to like it when they found out that she'd had to throw out four dozen of the best rolls this side of the Rockies just because he was being cranky? Not to mention the apple pies now cooling up at the house.

Zeke's eyes narrowed to slits. It had probably been seventy years since anyone had dared to label him cranky. Cantankerous, maybe. Or a few other, less polite words, but not cranky. Small children were cranky. He gave Megan a glare that had been known to make cowboys find urgent business elsewhere. Megan met the look without flinching and held out the big bowl. The smell of fresh bread wafted through the towel that covered it.

Zeke's mouth watered. He hadn't had fresh bread since the last time that old biddy of a housekeeper had brought some down. Gun had been talking up the new housekeeper's baking, saying she made the best pies he'd ever set a tooth to. If the men found out he'd turned her away—and he had a feeling she'd make sure they did find out—he was likely to have a riot on his hands. Besides, those rolls smelled mighty good.

"I don't give out my recipes," he snapped.

"Fine. Then maybe next time you make venison stew, you could make enough extra for the house. And when I have extra baking, I'll bring it down."

He nodded, accepting a fair trade. He made venison stew the next night and Megan kept the men supplied with fresh bread and baked pies or cakes a couple of times a week. Kel shook his head over her managing to get around Zeke, and the men became her instant friends.

Carey Wills and Dick Brownwell made room for her at the fence as Megan reached the corral. She wasn't sure what she'd expected to see, maybe one of the cowboys riding a bucking horse, but there was nothing in the corral except Kel and a bay horse, and they didn't seem to be doing anything but simply standing there.

"Kel's whispering him," Dick said, pitching his voice low.

"Whispering him?" She could see that Kel was talking to the young horse.

"Only ever seen one other fellow could whisper a horse the way the boss can." That was Carey, his weathered face full of admiration.

"What does it mean?" Megan asked without taking her eyes from Kel.

"He's talkin' that little fella into thinking it might be real nice to have a man on his back," Carey said. "Most folks break a horse by showin' 'em they can't be throwed. Sooner or later, the horse figures out there ain't nothin' so terrible about carryin' somebody around and they give up buckin' and fightin'."

"Doesn't Kel do that?"

Kel was stroking his hand over the young horse's neck, a slow, rhythmic motion that was hypnotic to watch.

"He's been known to ride a bronc with the best of 'em," Carey said. "But this little fella is one of Dude's get, and the boss has plans for him. So he's whispering him. Makes one of the best damn—beggin' your pardon, ma'am—ridin' horses you're ever like to swing a leg over."

"What does he say?" Megan found herself mesmerized by the motion of Kel's hand on the horse. Waves of energy seemed to shimmer from the center of the corral where the two of them stood.

"Nobody but the horse knows," Dick said. "Can't just anybody whisper one, either. You've got to have the right feel or touch or something. I'd heard about such things but never believed it until I saw the boss do it."

He continued, but Megan had lost track of what he was saying. Watching Kel, she could almost feel the pressure of his hand on her skin, hear the low rumble of his voice. She felt as if her bones were melting, all her fears slipping away. As if he was whispering her as well as the colt.

As if feeling her gaze on him, Kel's head lifted, his eyes finding her where she stood on the other side of the fence. Megan felt the impact of that look from her head to her heels, like a long, shivering stroke down her back. Kel didn't speak, only looked at her, and her heart was thumping against her breastbone, heat was pooling between her thighs, spreading outward to encompass her entire body until she was on fire.

She had no idea how long she stood there, transfixed, conscious only of those deep green eyes touching her. It was the colt who broke the spell. Surprised to find himself suddenly being ignored, he snorted and nudged Kel's shoulder. Kel turned to him and Megan drew a shuddering breath.

She glanced around self-consciously, sure that the cowboys must have seen what had happened, that the electricity that had sizzled between her and their boss must have created visible arcs in the still air. But no one was looking at her oddly. They were still watching Kel and the young horse. The whole exchange must have been over in a matter of seconds, she realized.

She backed away from the fence, half surprised to find that her legs would support her. Turning, she walked up to the house, feeling as if she'd been battered by a windstorm.

Chapter 7

The storm still hadn't broken by dinner. The clouds had drifted down out of the mountains, but they seemed to simply press the hot air closer to the ground, making it difficult to breathe. Occasional gusts of wind spun dust devils in the yard and rustled the leaves of the big elms that sheltered the house.

No one had much to say during the meal. Colleen was quiet, as she usually was in Gun's presence. More than once, Megan saw the girl sneaking looks at him across the table, such a tangle of emotions in her eyes that it was impossible to decipher any of them. A couple of times, Gun looked up as if sensing her gaze, but Colleen's glance would dart away before their eyes could meet. The regret in Gun's face was easy enough to read.

Megan thought again that she should try to get to the bottom of whatever was going on between the two of them, but her thoughts couldn't focus on the problem tonight. In fact, her thoughts couldn't focus on much of anything tonight. They skipped around like a grasshopper in a field of daisies, nibbling here and there but never stopping long enough for her to catch hold of one.

She was vividly aware of Kel sitting at the head of the table but she was careful to avoid looking at him, afraid of what her eyes might reveal. She was still shaken by the impact of the look they'd exchanged this afternoon. She was almost grateful when he disappeared into his study right after dinner.

The restlessness stayed with Megan as she cleaned the kitchen and made her plans for the next day's meals. Colleen was watching television in the living room but Megan wasn't in the mood to listen to canned laughter so she said good-night and went upstairs to her room. Her eyes lingered on the bar of light that showed beneath the door of Kel's study as she passed it.

Too restless to settle down with a book, she took a long, cool shower, letting the water sluice over her body. By the time she stepped into her bedroom, the storm had broken and the rain had finally begun to fall. It should have eased the tension, but Megan didn't feel any more relaxed than she had before her shower.

She pulled on a knee-length white cotton nightgown and brushed her hair until it crackled around the brush. Then she went to stand next to the window, watching the rain stream past, letting her thoughts drift where they would. Standing there, she lost track of time, and she was shocked to see how late it was when she finally turned and looked at the clock. It was past time she was getting to bed. But her gaze drifted to the door.

Had Kel come up? Or was he still downstairs? And what difference did it make to her, unless she was thinking of going to his room, which she wasn't.

Was she?

Kel stood in front of the window, watching the rain. Ranching, like farming, was largely dependent on regular rainfall. The Lazy B was in a better position than most, with a couple of sources of water that hadn't failed in the last hundred years or so, but plentiful rains meant good grass and good grass meant fat cattle that brought a better price on the market.

But Kel wasn't thinking about cattle prices or what the rain meant for the grass those cattle fed on. His thoughts weren't on the range, they were much closer to home. Just across the hall, in fact.

Was Megan asleep? Or was she lying awake watching the rain? Was she thinking about him? The look they'd exchanged this afternoon had damn near shattered his control. If they hadn't been standing under the blazing sun with half a dozen of his cowboys watching, he'd have had her right then and there. No more frustration, no more cold showers, no more waiting.

He'd told her that the decision was hers, that he wouldn't push. He'd been a damned fool. She wanted him. He could smell it as surely as he could smell the sweet, musty scent of the rain soaking into the dry ground outside. She could be his tonight. All he had to do was walk across the hall and she'd be his for the taking.

But he'd given his word and he wasn't quite ready to admit that he wanted her so much he'd break his promise. He didn't like that his hunger was powerful enough to make him even consider the idea. He didn't want to want her quite so much.

Lightning forked over the prairie, and Kel automatically counted the seconds until he heard the rumble of thunder. Ten miles or more. It would be a little while before the center of the storm reached them. There'd be plenty—

Some small sound reached him, and he felt the skin across the back of his shoulders tighten with sudden awareness. She was here. She'd entered with the thunder, the sound drowning out the click of the door latch. But he didn't need to hear her or even see her. He could feel her.

The thought that he was so attuned to her might have worried him if he'd given it much consideration, but he wasn't in a contemplative mood at the moment. He turned slowly. He'd left only one small lamp burning beside the bed, and the pool of its light fell far short of where Megan stood, but Kel's eyes were adjusted to the dimness, and he had no trouble seeing her. She was standing against the door, her white gown and pale hair stark against the dark wood.

She stayed where she was, letting her eyes adjust to the light. Looking for him. He could see her teeth worrying her lower lip and knew how difficult it had been for her to come to him. He heard her soft little catch of breath when she saw him, heard it change to a gasp of shock when lightning slashed across the window behind him and she realized that he wore not a stitch of clothing.

Thunder rolled across the room, and he had her in his arms before the echo of it faded, sweeping her up against his already aroused body, his mouth swallowing her startled cry. For the space of half a heartbeat, she was stiff in his hold, and then she seemed to dissolve against him, her slender body pliant and giving.

Wrapping his arms around her, Kel lifted her off the floor, crushing her against his hard frame. His tongue plunged into her mouth, tangling with hers, tasting her response, tasting her hunger.

By the time he'd walked with her to the bed, he could feel the breath shuddering in and out of her. Her fingers were wound in his hair, her back arched to press the fullness of her breasts against his chest. Kel flattened one hand across her bottom, lifting her up so that the soft core of her cradled his erection.

Lightning exploded outside, closer now, the thunder rumbling on its heels, drowning out the roar of his heartbeat, swallowing Megan's soft cry of surprise as he eased her legs apart, sliding his aching flesh between her thighs, supporting her so that she straddled him. The slick moisture of her arousal soothed even as it made the ache worse.

He tortured them both by easing his hips back, then forward again, a teasing hint of what was to come. Megan's head fell back, her breath leaving her on a sob. He could see the taut thrust of her breasts against the fabric of her nightgown. There was something wildly erotic about holding her like this, a heartbeat away from completing their joining, and seeing her still clothed in prim white cotton.

He felt her knee lift against his hip and knew that he could have her right here, those long legs wrapping around his hips as he lowered her onto his arousal. He let the image roll through his mind as his hand slid downward, drawing her knee higher on his hip, his fingertips brushing the damp curls at the juncture of her thighs. He felt the shiver that ran through her at the light touch. He'd known it would be like this with her, known the passion would explode between them, known how she'd respond to his touch.

With a soft groan of regret, Kel eased her down. The hunger was too great this time, too powerful for him to try anything exotic. Later, he promised himself as he dragged the nightgown over her head. Once the initial hunger was slaked, there'd be time for him to fulfill every fantasy he'd had during these endless weeks of waiting and wanting. But this first time, he wanted her stretched out beneath him, her hair spread across his pillow, just the way he'd imagined her a hundred times.

Megan whispered his name as he eased her onto the bed, following her down, the thick mat of hair on his chest abrading her swollen nipples. Kel wanted to taste her there, wanted to let his tongue explore the indentation of her belly button, wanted to taste the slick dampness between her thighs, to hear her cries of pleasure as he brought her to a peak with his mouth and tongue.

But Megan parted her legs, those legs that were much too long for a woman her size, the ones that had haunted his nights ever since they met. Lightning lit the room as her knees came up on either side of his hips, her soft whimpers urging him to complete their union.

Later, Kel promised himself. Promised her. Later, there'd be time for everything else. This first time, the hunger was too great, the need too powerful. This first time, there was no room for anything but slaking the elemental hunger that gnawed at both of them.

He caught one of her hands in his, lowering her fingers to where their bodies almost joined. In the darkness, he saw her eyes widen as her fingers closed around him as if she was surprised by the size of him. Well, he was damn near surprised himself, Kel thought with painful humor. He'd never been so achingly aroused in his life. Just the touch of her small fingers nearly sent him over the edge.

Any uncertainty she felt was only momentary. She eased him forward, and Kel thought he'd surely die from the pleasure as he felt her soft folds yield before the blunt pressure of his erection.

Heat and dampness enfolded him. He closed his eyes and ground his teeth together as he eased himself deeper into her soft sheath. She was so small and tight. So tight. Almost as if he was the first man to know her like this. Almost as if she— His eyes flew open at the thought, and he stared at her, reading the uncertainty behind the need, the flicker of fear behind the hunger.

"You're a virgin." The words hovered somewhere between statement and accusation.

"It doesn't matter." Her short fingernails dug into the firm muscles of his buttocks, urging him deeper. "Don't stop," she whispered frantically. "Please, Kel. Don't stop."

"Stop?" His laugh ended with a pained groan. "Hell, woman, do you think I'm made of stone?"

He was most definitely not made of stone. Megan was sure of that if not much else at the moment. He was tight skin over hard muscles. He was the crisp brush of chest hair over the almost painfully sensitive skin of her breasts. He was a heavy pressure building inside her. But he was most definitely not stone.

She was trembling with a sudden, completely unexpected and purely feminine fear. He was so much bigger than she was, stronger, more powerful. There was something a little frightening about that strength, that power. For a panicked second, she wanted to tell him she'd changed her mind. She wanted to slide off the big bed and flee to the safety of her room. But the thought of stopping, of not finding out what lay at the end of this path she'd started out on, was more than she could bear.

"Please," she whispered against his throat. She hardly knew what she was asking for.

At the sound of her plea, she felt Kel still against her, and for an instant she was afraid he was going to stop after all. With a whimpered protest, she arched her hips, taking him deeper. Kel groaned, a low guttural sound of pleasure.

"Easy," he whispered against her temple. His voice was hardly audible over the hiss of the rain outside. "There's no need to rush."

There was a need. She was burning up inside, trembling against him. Kel caught hold of her arms, sliding his hands down until his fingers were wrapped around hers. Megan murmured a protest as he pressed them to the pillow on either side of her head.

"Look at me."

As if she had a choice. His eyes glittered green in the thin lamplight, and Megan had the odd feeling that it would be possible to lose her soul in those eyes. But it wasn't her soul that concerned her at the moment.

His gaze locked with hers, his hands still holding hers, Kel flexed his hips forward, completing their union with one heavy thrust, filling her emptiness with his solid presence. Megan forgot how to breathe.

She'd thought that there was no real mystery. She knew the mechanics of it, knew what went where, knew that everything was designed to fit together, though she'd experienced a few doubts on that score when she'd felt the size of him. But despite that momentary hesitation, she thought she knew exactly what to expect.

She was wrong.

Nothing could have prepared her for the incredible feeling of invasion, the sensation of her body stretching to accommodate Kel's, of sharing herself so intimately with a man. With an inarticulate sound that could have been protest, could have been welcome, she arched beneath him, not sure whether she was trying to throw him off or take him deeper.

Kel groaned, a low, tortured sound from between clenched teeth, as he sank fully within her. She was as tight as a glove around him, all heat and dampness. He felt the faint ripple of tiny muscles as they adjusted to his presence. It was a sweet torment.

She gasped as he eased back, then slid forward again. He saw the startled pleasure in her eyes just before the lids dropped. He lowered his mouth to hers, drinking in her soft moans, tasting them more than hearing them. The storm seemed to have stopped directly over the house, and the sound of the rain was a constant roar. Or was that the blood rushing in his ears?

Lightning flashed almost continuously, illuminating the two figures on the wide bed. Kel had left the window open a crack, and the smell of rain and damp earth mixed with the musky scent of sweat and sex. Kel's big body arched over Megan's slender form, his slow, steady movements becoming less measured as she struggled for control of the moment, struggled for the release she could sense just out of reach.

Tension coiled inside her, tightening with every move Kel made until she felt as if she might burst. The pleasure was so intense it hovered on the knife edge of pain. There was something, something she couldn't quite... Kel slid his hands under her, his fingers digging into her bottom as he lifted her into his thrusts, controlling the rhythm, controlling her uncertain movements, giving her what she sought.

A bolt of lightning ripped through the air just outside the window. As the fierce, blue-white light slashed across the room, Megan saw Kel's face above her, the skin tight across his cheekbones, his eyes a glitter of green. And then the tension within her snapped abruptly, and the resultant waves of pleasure convulsed her body.

Thunder crashed a heartbeat after the lightning, and the house rocked with the force of it. Or was it the bed rocking with the force of their loving? Megan neither knew nor cared. Instinctively, she brought her knees up on either side of his hips, taking him deeper still, as her short nails dug into the taut muscles of his back. And then Kel was shuddering in her arms, his harsh groan of fulfillment all but drowned out by the sound of the storm.

It was a long time before Kel gained enough breath to ease himself away from Megan. Her faint murmur could have been protest or good riddance, but there was no mistaking the way her fingers clung to his shoulders.

"I'm not going far," he whispered, half surprised he was still capable of putting together a coherent sentence.

Surely, the intensity of what had passed between them must have burned out a few synapses in his brain. True to his word, he didn't go far. As he settled on the bed, his arm was already around Megan, pulling her close against his side.

They lay quietly, listening to the storm outside, though it seemed but a pale imitation of the storm that had just raged between the two of them. Kel stroked damp tendrils of pale hair from Megan's forehead, only a little surprised to see that his fingers were not quite steady.

He was stunned by the force of what had just happened. He'd never experienced anything quite like it, as if everything he was, both body and soul, had been poured into that one moment. Kel shied away from that thought, not caring for the direction it could take him.

"Are you all right?" he whispered huskily.

She nodded without lifting her head from where it rested on his shoulder. Her fingers curled in the thick mat of dark hair on his chest.

"Why now? Why me?" He felt tension creep through her lax body and half wished he hadn't said anything. But as the sensual fog started to lift from his mind, he found himself wondering why she'd chosen him to be her first lover.

And not sure he wanted to hear the answer.

Megan didn't pretend not to know what Kel was asking. She felt the subtle tension in him and knew her answer was important. What could she tell him? That she thought she might be falling in love with him? She didn't need to be psychic to know that he didn't want to hear that. Besides, she wasn't sure of her feelings, she told herself, half afraid she was lying.

"It felt right," she said finally, glad their positions meant that she didn't have to meet his eyes.

"It felt right?" Kel rolled that thought around for a moment. He should be relieved. God forbid she should announce that she loved him. He didn't need or want those kinds of promises. He'd had them once before and had quickly learned how hollow they could be. He was glad that Megan didn't feel the need to wrap their attraction up in pretty, emotional bows.

Still, "it felt right" didn't seem like much of a reason for a twenty-five-year-old virgin to decide to sleep with a man. It ought to mean more than that, he thought, aware of feeling a little disgruntled.

But it wasn't any of his business why she'd made the choice she had. As long as she didn't expect more from him than he could give, then her reasons didn't make any difference to him. None at all.

Her fingers brushed across a flat nipple hidden in the thick mat of chest hair, and though it hardly seemed possible after the explosive lovemaking they'd just shared, Kel felt a stir of arousal. Megan couldn't avoid feeling it also, considering the intimacy of her leg thrown across his hips.

She laughed, a low, throaty sound that made his blood thicken and his skin heat. He moved suddenly, hearing her gasp as he shifted her to lie on top of him, her slender body pressed the length of his much harder frame. After a startled moment, she moved slightly, adjusting to the new position.

Kel barely stifled a groan as the softness of her belly pressed more firmly against his hardening flesh. He couldn't remember ever wanting a woman like this. He'd just had her, yet his body was responding as if it had been months since he'd touched a woman.

He slid his hands up the length of her, easing his thumbs under the weight of her breasts, brushing them across the sensitive nipples while his mouth was busy exploring the skin beneath her ear.

"If I'd known this was so much fun, maybe I wouldn't have waited so long," she said breathlessly, her skin heating under his hands.

Kel flattened one hand against her bottom, pressing her closer to his arousal. He didn't like the idea of Megan with another man—past or future. The thought made him want to sheath himself in her, to make love to her again and again until she was unmistakably branded as his, until she was incapable of so much as thinking of another man.

At another time, the fierceness of that thought might have given him pause, but he was somewhat preoccupied at the moment. Megan laughed again, that same breathy, sensuous sound that drove him wild. Kel gave up thinking completely, deciding that his time could be more profitably occupied elsewhere.

Megan measured coffee into the filter. There was a fine tremor in her fingers that made the simple task more difficult than it should have been. When she spilled coffee for the second time, she set down the scoop and leaned her hands on the edge of the counter. Taking a deep breath and then another, she tried to slow the quick beat of her heart.

Stop acting like an idiot, she scolded herself. What was the big deal about seeing Kel at breakfast? She'd been doing that every morning since she came to the Lazy B.

But this morning, he wasn't just her employer or even the man for whom she felt a powerful attraction. This morning he was her lover.

She swallowed and closed her eyes. It was silly to be so nervous. She hadn't been this nervous when she went to his room last night, she thought ruefully.

Maybe she shouldn't have crept to her bed in the gray hour just before dawn. If she'd stayed in his bed, awakened next to him, their first meeting would already be over with and she wouldn't be standing here shaking like a leaf at the thought of it.

But waking from a deep sleep, she'd lay there, listening to the sound of Kel's breathing, aware of him in ways she'd never known before, and it had suddenly seemed unbearably intimate. As if waking up beside the man was more intimate than having sex with him, she'd scoffed to herself. But she'd still slid out of bed and struggled into her nightgown before creeping from his room and fleeing to the safety of her own.

She should have stayed in bed, she thought. After all, Kel had made it clear from the start that breakfast was not part of her job. This morning, she should have taken that to heart and stayed in bed because she was suddenly absolutely positive that she couldn't face him.

Megan was so absorbed in her panicky thoughts that she completely missed hearing Kel's arrival until the solid click of his boot heels on the polished floor was right behind her. Before she could do more than gasp, his hands closed around her waist, turning her toward him. She caught a quick glimpse of the wicked grin that sparkled in his green eyes and then his mouth came down on hers.

Shock kept her rigid in Kel's arms, but only for a moment. The soft brush of his mustache against her upper lip and the warm persuasion of his tongue parting her mouth had her melting against him. She forgot how nervous she'd been about this meeting, forgot that they were standing in the middle of the kitchen where Colleen could walk in or one of the hands could come looking for Kel. Megan forgot everything but the feel of Kel's arms around her, the muscled length of his body against her and the taste of him on her mouth.

There was no telling how long the kiss might have lasted if the necessity for oxygen hadn't intruded. By the time Kel lifted his head, Megan could only cling to him, her hands fisted in his shirt, her eyes slightly glazed as she looked at him.

"Good morning." He smiled at her, looking very masculine and more than a little pleased with himself. An observer might have thought Kel unaffected by their embrace. But Megan was close enough to feel the rapid beat of his heart, not to mention the unmistakable pressure of his arousal against her belly.

"Good morning." She was surprised to hear how normal she sounded, particularly since Kel's hands were sliding down her back, arousing every nerve ending they passed over.

"What's for breakfast?"

"I was going to make pancakes." The last word ended on a squeak as his fingers closed over her bottom, lifting her off her feet.

"Good." Since he was nibbling the sensitive skin behind her ear, just what he was referring to was somewhat open to interpretation.

Megan's fingers slipped into the thick, dark hair at the back of his skull, her head tilting to allow him access to the arched line of her throat. Access of which he took full advantage, letting her feel the edge of his teeth along the taut skin. Then he dipped his tongue into the hollow at its base, tasting the frantic pulse that beat there. Megan tugged on his hair and he obliged her by bringing his mouth to hers for a ravenous kiss that stole what little breath she had left.

Not until he had melted nearly every bone in her body did he lift his head and let her slide to the floor. He let his hands linger on her waist, whether out of reluctance to release her or because he sensed that her knees wouldn't hold her, Megan could only guess. Perhaps it was the latter, because he turned her away from the counter, and pulling a chair out from the table with his foot, he settled her into it.

"I'll make breakfast." She nodded, completely incapable of a more articulate response. He started to turn away and then turned back, bending to drop a quick, hard kiss on her mouth. "We'll finish this tonight."

He didn't wait for a response before turning to the counter. Megan watched him finish measuring the coffee into the filter, her pulse still skittering wildly.

Tonight suddenly seemed a very long way away.

Chapter 8

Kel had a perfectly good reason for leaving the job he'd been doing and coming up to the house in the middle of the afternoon. He'd torn his shirt and wanted to change it. If he didn't, the tear was only going to get worse. No sense in ruining a perfectly good shirt.

If it hadn't been for catching his shirt on a nail, he wouldn't have set foot in the house until it was time to wash for dinner. The fact that he hadn't been able to get Megan out of his mind all morning had nothing to do with it. Not a thing. The fact that just thinking about his housekeeper's sweet curves and even sweeter response had him half hard and aching was irrelevant.

It was also irrelevant that he'd seen Colleen's physical therapist arrive, which meant that his little sister was going to be occupied for the next hour or so. He hadn't been looking for the woman's arrival, but he could hardly miss seeing a lipstick red compact car parked right in front of the house. Hell, a car that color was like a siren going off in a monastery.

Okay, maybe it had occurred to him that he might see Megan when he came up to the house. But that certainly hadn't been a driving factor in his decision to drop what he'd been doing and come inside. If it hadn't been for the shirt...

He'd have thought of something else.

The admission stung, even in the privacy of his own thoughts, slowing his stride as he stepped through the door and into the kitchen. The room was empty, and he wanted to believe he didn't feel a twinge of disappointment, just like he wanted to believe he hadn't trumped up an excuse to see Megan. But he wasn't quite that good at lying to himself.

He set his hat on the hook near the door and ran his fingers through his hair. Damn it all, this hunger was supposed to have been eased by sleeping with her! But they'd been lovers for over a week now and he wanted her more than ever. Since the night of the storm, she'd spent every night in his bed, in his arms. He should have been feeling relaxed, satiated. Instead he felt like a stallion who'd just caught the scent of a mare ready to be covered.

A quick search of the lower floor told him that Megan wasn't there. Kel started up the stairs, unbuttoning his torn shirt as he went. Every morning, she crept out of his bed in the gray hour before dawn and slipped across the hall to her room. And every morning, he feigned sleep, watching her through his lashes, half relieved that she was going. As if waking up next to her would somehow be even more intimate than having sex with her, he told himself with dark humor.

But ridiculous as it was, that's how it felt. So he let her think he was still asleep, torturing himself by watching as she tiptoed to wherever her nightgown had ended up the night before. Since it had generally been removed in the most expedient manner rather than the neatest, it always took her a moment to untangle the sleeves, giving Kel plenty of time to admire the delicate lines of her body in the predawn light that filtered through the room.

He always felt a stir of arousal, no matter how many times they'd made love the night before, no matter how impossible it seemed that he could want her yet again. When she lifted her arms to slide the nightgown over her head, he swallowed a groan at the perfect arch of her body. If he hadn't known better, he would have believed that she was deliberately tantalizing him, a striptease in reverse, allowing him a last glimpse of her body before leaving. But despite the fact that she was as passionate a lover as he could have wished for, there was still a streak of shyness in Megan. No, her teasing was purely unintentional and all the more effective because of it.

Each morning, he forced himself to stay where he was and let Megan creep from the room. And every morning, he immediately wanted to follow her, to pull her into his room, into his bed and keep her there for the rest of the day.

At breakfast, he'd look at her across the table and think about having her on her back on that same table, her pale hair scattered across the warm oak, his hands hooked under her shoulders to hold her still against the force of his thrusts. Thoughts like that had a tendency to make his first few minutes in the saddle a little uncomfortable.

With each day that passed, he found it harder and harder to put her out of his mind and concentrate on the work at hand. It seemed as if, no matter how many times he had her, he still wanted her. Like one of those rashes that, the more you scratched it, the more it itched, his hunger just got stronger. He doubted Megan would appreciate being compared to a rash, but the comparison, at least in terms of his own response, was apt. Which was why he found himself traipsing up to the house in the middle of the day on a trumped-up excuse.

Irritated with himself, Kel jerked his shirt off as he walked down the hall to his room. He was going to change his shirt and go right outside. It was one thing to have an affair with Megan, something else altogether to let her interfere with his work. With luck, she was cleaning a bathroom on the other side of the house. He could change and be gone without even seeing her.

He came to a dead stop in the doorway of his room. She was making his bed, bent over it, stretching a fresh sheet around the top of the mattress. Kel had a perfect view of the full curves of her bottom covered in soft denim. His fingers clenched on the shirt he held. His jeans were suddenly much too tight—a phenomenon that seemed to occur fairly often when she was around. And this time, he knew exactly what lay beneath that faded denim. The knowledge did nothing to ease the snugness of his jeans.

She stretched a little farther and the powder blue T-shirt she wore inched upward, baring a swath of pale skin. Kel bit back a groan as the constriction of his jeans threatened to become downright painful.

Damn. He had to get control of himself. He shouldn't be standing here in the middle of the day, with work waiting to be done, and all he could think about was tumbling his new housekeeper onto the half-made bed and making love to her until neither of them had the strength to get up.

Megan finished smoothing the sheet and without turning reached behind her for the top sheet, which she'd set on the night table. Her hand encountered bare skin and taut muscles instead.

She spun around, getting only a quick glimpse of Kel before she found her feet swept out from under her. She hit the bed with a muffled shriek, bouncing slightly on the firm mattress. She just had time to draw a breath before he came down on top of her. He tugged at the hem of her T-shirt.

"What are you doing?" she demanded, trying to ignore the shivers of awareness rippling over her skin.

"I'm ravishing you." He sounded surprised that she'd had to ask. Megan giggled, shoving ineffectually at his marauding hands.

"It's broad daylight."

"The best time for ravishment." He succeeded in shoving her T-shirt up under her arms and flicked open the front clasp on her bra.

"We can't," she muttered, feeling her nipples tighten in anticipation.

"Why not?" He bent to nuzzle her breast.

"It's broad daylight."

"You're repeating yourself." He opened his mouth over her nipple, scoring it gently with his teeth before laving it with his tongue. Megan's breath grew ragged as he repeated the treatment on the other breast. Only when both nipples had been drawn to pebble hardness did he lift his head.

"Of course if you *really* want me to go," he murmured.

"Try it and I'll put ground glass in your stew tonight. Do you know what ground glass does to your stomach?"

She pushed him onto his back and straddled his hips, though she knew it was only because he allowed it. If he hadn't wanted to move, she could have pushed from now until next week and not budged him an inch.

"Actually, I don't," he said, his attention less on the conversation than on the feel of her fingers fumbling with his belt buckle.

"You don't want to know."

"I've got my boots on the clean sheet," he pointed out as the buckle slid open.

"I'll change it again." The zipper yielded and she slid her hand inside the fabric of his shorts. Kel sucked a breath between his teeth as her fingers closed around him.

"Damn, you're likely to kill me."

"Of course, if you *really* want me to go," she murmured. She loosened her fingers and shifted as if to get off him.

Kel's hands closed like a vise around her hips, holding her in place. "I wouldn't try it, if I were you. No telling what might happen to a woman who teased a man like that."

"I thought a woman was always safe in the West," she said breathlessly.

"Only as safe as she wants to be," he said, his voice raspy. "Now, if you'll shut up, I'd like to continue with this ravishment."

The dangerous smile in her eyes and the downright wicked movement of her hands made it obvious that plan suited her just fine.

"What are you looking at?" Megan asked Colleen as she stepped out onto the porch.

She'd just finished loading the dishwasher after dinner. Kel had disappeared into his study and she'd been on her way up to her room to read—or so she'd told herself. In reality, she'd probably sit there with an open, unread book in her lap while her thoughts wandered to their favorite topic these days, which was Kel.

After three weeks as his lover, she could no longer fool herself into thinking that she *might* be in love with him. Honesty compelled her to admit that she'd gone right past might and was well on her way to head over heels.

She'd spent more than enough time thinking about Kel Bryan, wondering how he felt, wondering if she was heading for a broken heart at the end of the summer. When she'd seen Colleen standing on the porch, Megan had decided that she'd much rather talk to Colleen than contemplate the unsettled state of her life.

At the sound of Megan's voice, Colleen jumped and jerked around to face her, looking as guilty as if she'd been caught spying through a peephole.

"Nothing," she said quickly, defensively.

Her brows going up a little, Megan looked in the direction the girl had been facing.

Three cowboys stood near the corral. The sun had almost disappeared behind the western mountains, and in the blue-purple light that remained, the men were little more than silhouettes. They could have been cowboys from any place, any time, identifiable by the tilt of their hats and the unique stance caused by wearing pointy-toed boots better suited to a stirrup than the ground.

Then one of them straightened away from the fence and reached up to take off his hat. Even in this light, there was no mistaking the pale color of his hair. That and his size identified him as easily as if he'd been standing under a floodlight.

"That's Gun, isn't it?"

"Could be." Colleen shrugged and turned her back on the scene, making her indifference plain.

Megan glanced from the girl's set face to the tall cowboy, her expression speculative. She'd been here more than a month, and she was no closer to understanding what was going on between Colleen and Gun than she had been that first day. Colleen still avoided looking at him, rarely spoke to him and continued to come up with thin excuses for leaving any room he entered. And Gun still looked at her with regret, as if viewing something he'd once valued and then lost.

"What's going on between you and Gun?" she asked bluntly.

Colleen jerked as if Megan had struck her. Her green eyes, so like her brother's, were wide and startled. "I don't know what you mean."

"It's none of my business, of course," Megan said as she turned so that she could lean against the porch railing. She folded her arms across her chest and looked at the younger woman. "But I can't help but notice that you practically run every time Gun comes into sight. And if you can't escape, you avoid looking at him and talking to him."

"I do not," Colleen protested, even as guilty color rose in her cheeks.

"Yes, you do. Like I said, it's none of my business." Megan shrugged. "But I've begun to think of you as a friend these last few weeks and I hate to see you so unhappy."

"I think of you as a friend, too. I...I don't have too many of those these days." She rubbed her injured leg absently. "It's partly my fault, I guess. After... after I got hurt, I didn't feel much like seeing anybody. I guess I wasn't very tactful about saying so. I really like you," Colleen admitted with a shy smile that went straight to Megan's heart.

"I really like you, too." Acting on impulse, she put her arms around Colleen and gave her a quick hug. She had to blink to clear her vision when she stepped

back. In the light from the porch lamp, Colleen's eyes
seemed suspiciously bright, too.

"If I didn't like you, I wouldn't poke my nose in
where it doesn't belong," Megan said briskly, bringing the conversation back to her original question.
"What's going on between you and Gun?"

"Nothing." Colleen's eyes slid past her to where
Gun stood with the other two cowboys. Her eyes held
more sadness than any nineteen-year-old's had a right
to.

"You can tell me to mind my own business and I'll
leave you alone, but don't try to tell me there's nothing going on," Megan said sternly.

"It's the truth." Colleen caught Megan's eye. "It's
kind of the truth."

"I think that's like being kind of dead. It's either the
truth or it's not, and I'm betting on the not."

She wouldn't have pressed so hard if she hadn't had
the feeling that Colleen desperately needed to talk to
someone. Kel adored his little sister, and Megan knew
he'd move heaven and earth if he thought it would
help her, but since he and Gun were friends, maybe
Colleen felt awkward about talking to him.

"Colleen, Gun hasn't... I mean, it's not that he
ever... scared you in any way, is it?" She'd come to
know and like Gun, and she couldn't stretch her
imagination to encompass him doing anything to harm
any woman, even if she hadn't been his best friend's
sister. Still, she felt the question had to be asked.

"Scared me?" Colleen looked puzzled for a moment and then her eyes widened in shock. She took a
step back and sank down into a wicker chair, looking

as if she'd just received a body blow. "You think he tried to...that Gun might have..."

"I don't think anything," Megan said carefully. "But if it was something like that, I want you to know that you could tell me about it."

"It wasn't anything like that." There could be no doubting the sincerity behind Colleen's vehement denial. "Gun would never... I mean, he couldn't possibly..." She broke off, pressing her palms to her flushed cheeks.

"I had to ask."

"I...I understand, but it wasn't that. Good grief, even if he'd thought about—which he never would—he knows, everybody knows, Kel would kill anybody who hurt me."

"I figured as much." Kel was very protective of what was his, Megan thought a little wistfully. She'd have given a great deal to be able to think that he considered her his for more than just the summer.

"It's nothing Gun did," Colleen said slowly. "He's been Kel's friend for as long as I can remember. His mother died when he was little, and Gun and his father, they never got along, so Gun used to spend a lot of time here. He was like another brother to me." The way her eyes shifted and the flush that came up in her cheeks made Megan suspect that "brother" didn't quite describe Gun's place in the girl's heart but she nodded as if accepting the statement at face value. "It's my fault that we're not friends anymore. I...said things, terrible things."

"Friendships are pretty resilient," Megan said gently. "Maybe—"

But Colleen was already shaking her head. "I couldn't ask him to forgive me. I can't even forgive myself."

"Why don't you tell me what happened?"

Colleen hesitated a moment before speaking. "Gun was with me when I got hurt."

Megan was surprised. It had never occurred to her that Colleen's avoidance of Gun had anything to do with her injury.

"We'd already had some snow but there was a chinook right after New Year's and most of the snow had melted. The temperature dropped almost immediately but it didn't snow. I hadn't gone back to school yet and I wanted to get out of the house. Kel was busy but he didn't want me going out alone so Gun said he'd go riding with me." Her eyes looked through Megan and into the past.

"I took my mare out. Spooky. I'd raised her and trained her myself. We did some barrel racing last summer. She had...she had the softest mouth and she could turn on a dime and give back nine cents change."

Colleen's hands twisted together in her lap, her voice choked with emotion. Megan felt guilty about having forced her to relive what was obviously a very painful time.

"Gun said we might as well check on a couple of stock tanks while we were curing my cabin fever. It was cold and the footing wasn't the best. The snow had melted into mud and then, when the temperature dropped, the top layer of mud froze.

"Spooky was full of energy after being cooped up in the barn and she wanted to run but the ground was too muddy. We'd checked one stock tank and were on our way to look at another one when Spooky acted up, prancing and bobbing her head. She just wanted to run." Colleen's voice broke but she seemed oblivious to the tear that slid down her pale cheek.

"What happened?"

"She slipped. We were on the edge of a wash but it would have been all right if the ground hadn't been so slick. She went over the edge."

"And you went with her."

"I didn't kick free fast enough. It wasn't a deep wash but she fell so hard. I was still dazed when Gun got to us. My leg was trapped and Spooky... Spooky was trying to get up. She calmed when Gun spoke to her but she'd... she'd broken her leg. I could see how bad it was but I wouldn't believe it. I guess I was in shock. I couldn't even feel my own leg." She rubbed her fingers over her left leg as if soothing a deep ache.

"Gun... Gun had a gun with him. Some of the hands carry them when they're out on the range. He... he did what he had to do." She shook her head as if to clear the echo of the shot from her ears.

Megan wiped away the dampness on her own cheeks and moved to sit in the glider that hung near Colleen's chair, reaching over to take one of the girl's hands in hers. Colleen's fingers clung to her as if grateful for the contact.

"He didn't have any choice," she said, her voice hardly more than a whisper. "I know that. I think, even then, I knew it. But I screamed at him. I called him a murderer.''

''You were hurt. You'd just lost a friend. I'm sure Gun knew you didn't mean it.''

''I did mean it at the time. I hated him right then.''

''That's not so hard to understand. I can't believe he'd hold it against you all these months later.''

''Maybe not, but there's more. Gun pulled me free. My leg was pretty bad but I wasn't feeling it yet. It was too cold for him to risk leaving me there while he went for help so he used his shirt and a couple of old boards he found and immobilized my leg as best he could. And then he put me on his horse and brought me home. I passed out before we got here.''

''I'm not surprised,'' Megan said dryly, thinking of the kind of pain she must have endured. Her fingers tightened over Colleen's, offering sympathy.

''When Gun came to visit me in the hospital, they'd just told me how bad my leg was. I overheard one of the nurses say it was a pity I'd always limp. When I saw Gun, I was boiling inside with fear and anger. I blamed him for the accident and Spooky's death and said it was his fault that my leg was such a mess. I...I told him I'd never forgive him for making me a cripple,'' she finished in a shamed whisper.

Megan was silent a moment, digesting the story Colleen had told her. She glanced toward the corral. It was dark now, but there was enough of a moon for her to make out Gun's tall figure. He was alone, his arms on the top rail of the fence as he stared into the darkness. She thought of the impression she'd had that there was something haunting him, that he carried a loneliness deep inside himself.

"Do you blame him?" she asked after a moment. "Do you think it was his fault?"

"Of course not!" Colleen sounded shocked. "I was just hurt and scared and I lashed out at him, but I knew, even then, that it wasn't his fault. If it hadn't been for Gun, I'd have died."

"Did you tell him that?"

Colleen shook her head, lowering her eyes to her fingers, which were twisted together in her lap. "I've been so ashamed of the way I acted, I can't even look Gun in the eye. He must despise me."

Megan shook her head, remembering the look in Gun's eyes when Colleen left the room to avoid him. "I don't think so."

"I don't see how he could help it."

"Maybe he thinks you really *do* blame him for the accident. Maybe he thinks you avoid him because you hold him to blame for it."

"He couldn't think that." Colleen shook her head in denial. "He knows it wasn't his fault."

"Maybe. But does he know *you* know that? You never told him you knew you were wrong."

"But he *must* know," Colleen protested.

"How?"

"Well, because . . . because he just *has* to know."

"How?" Megan repeated, gentle but implacable.

"I . . . I don't know. . . ." Colleen's voice trailed off in a whisper.

"Maybe you should tell him," Megan suggested quietly. "Maybe you owe him that much," she added, forestalling the protest she saw in Colleen's eyes.

Colleen looked past her, and Megan didn't have to turn to know that Gun was still standing by the corral. The look in the girl's eyes, half wistful, half scared, made it obvious.

"What would I say?" The question was asked of herself more than Megan, but Megan chose to answer it anyway.

"You'll find the right words."

She certainly hoped she hadn't made a huge mistake, Megan thought as she watched Colleen cross the yard to where Gun stood. The girl's awkward limp was a reminder that she'd already suffered more than most people twice her age.

What if she'd been wrong about Gun? Megan chewed on her lower lip as Colleen stopped a little way behind him. She must have said something, because the tall figure turned away from the fence, and Megan didn't think it was her imagination that made the movement look startled. The two of them stood there for a moment, and Megan held her breath. Gun moved away from the fence, and he and Colleen disappeared into the deep shadow cast by the barn.

Megan relaxed, allowing the pent-up breath to escape. At least he hadn't rejected her out of hand. If they'd just talk to each other, she was sure they could work things out.

A burst of laughter drifted up from the bunkhouse, and somewhere far away a coyote yipped, the sound escalating into a mournful howl. It was one of

Megan's favorite times of day. She was still caught off guard by the utter stillness of the Wyoming nights, by the thick darkness of the sky and the brilliance of the stars strewn across it.

She pushed her toe against the floor and set the glider in motion. For the first time since she'd left her grandparents' farm, Megan felt as if she'd found a place she could stay. This place spoke to her in a way no other place ever had. There was a stark beauty to the land that seemed to feed something in her soul.

At the end of summer, when Grace Cavenaugh reclaimed her job, Megan thought she might stay. Not on the Lazy B, of course, unless Kel invited her to do so, and it was dangerous to let herself even consider that possibility.

"Is that Gun with Colleen?"

Megan had been so absorbed in her thoughts that she hadn't heard Kel's approach until he spoke. She jumped slightly, sending a quick shiver through the glider. Turning her head, she saw him standing just inside the screen, which explained why she hadn't heard the door open. He pushed the door open and stepped out onto the porch, his eyes looking past her.

He was wearing a pair of clean but faded jeans and a black T-shirt that molded every muscle of his shoulders. He'd exchanged boots for a pair of soft-soled moccasins. With his dark hair, tanned skin and with the lamp casting angled shadows across his face, he looked as much Indian as cowboy. From there, it was a relatively short step to wondering what he'd look like wearing a breechclout.

"Is that Gun with Colleen?" Kel asked again, interrupting the lascivious turn her thoughts had taken.

Megan followed his gaze and saw the two figures who'd emerged from the shadow of the barn and were making their way slowly toward the house. Gun's arm was slung around the girl's shoulders, his long stride slowed to accommodate her awkward gait.

"That's Gun with Colleen," Megan confirmed, feeling her heart swell with pleasure and a healthy dollop of relief. If she'd been wrong about Gun's reaction... But she hadn't been, and this had proved to be one of those rare occasions when a little meddling was a good thing. Not that she'd really done anything...

"What did you do?" Kel's question made her flush a little, but she didn't pretend not to know what he meant.

"Not much, really. Colleen and I talked and I suggested that she might want to talk to Gun."

Kel gave her a disbelieving look. "After six months of her acting like a scared rabbit around him, that's all it took?"

"I think the time was right."

Kel sat down on the glider, angling his long body so that his knee just brushed hers. Megan knew she had it pretty bad when even that casual touch sent a tingle of awareness up her spine.

"You've been good for Colleen," he said. "I think she needed a friend."

"So did I," Megan said quietly.

Gun and Colleen reached the porch just then, and Kel turned to speak to Gun, looking as if there was nothing extraordinary about seeing his best friend and his little sister walking together.

Sitting there, with the glider moving idly beneath him and Megan's knee just brushing his, Kel was aware of a feeling of lazy contentment, a vague sense of peace. Through the back of his mind drifted the thought that Colleen wasn't the only one Megan had been good for. But he shied away from considering that idea too closely.

Chapter 9

The sun shone down out of a pale blue August sky.
Megan straightened from where she'd been crouched
between the rows of green beans and arched her back
to stretch the cramped muscles. Closing her eyes, she
turned her face so the sun could find its way under the
brim of the bright red baseball cap she wore. She sa-
vored the feel of its heat pouring over her. It wouldn't
be all that long before winter made this kind of
warmth a distant memory.

Megan shivered, her mood of sun worship abruptly
spoiled. Opening her eyes, she stared down the row of
beans, twined up head-high trellises on either side of
her. The big kitchen garden was one of her favorite
places on the ranch. She enjoyed all of it, but she'd
watched with particular delight the growth of this neat
green tunnel, tracking the progress of the bean plants
up the web of strings stretched between sturdy poles.

They'd started out as ankle-high streaks of green, the tiny plants looking somewhat ridiculous in comparison to the tall trellis they were expected to cover. But cover it they had.

Spotting a bean she'd missed, she reached out and pulled it free with a quick twist of the wrist. Zeke, the bunkhouse cook, had taken great pains to show her the right way to pick a string bean, a skill he seemed to think took some practice to master. Megan had listened and watched, giving the lesson the attention he clearly felt it deserved. She had come to like the crusty old buzzard, though she couldn't have said just why.

Instead of dropping the bean into the enamel pot at her feet, Megan nipped the stem end off with the edge of her thumbnail and bit into the crisp, sun-warmed flesh. From where she stood, she could see the ranch house, perfectly framed by the green walls on either side of her. It was a beautiful picture. The house looked solid, as if it had been here a long time and had every intention of being here a great deal longer.

Megan sighed and reached out to twist another bean from the plant, dropping it absently into the bowl at her feet. The house had good reason to be confident of its place, she thought whimsically. Unfortunately, she didn't.

Grace Cavenaugh's daughter had been delivered of a healthy baby girl three weeks ago. The new grandmother was staying on to help her daughter get on her feet. She hadn't mentioned just how much longer she expected to be away from the Lazy B, but Megan doubted it would be more than two or three weeks at most. Then Gracie would return to her job.

And I'll be out of one.

Not that she gave a damn about the job. If that had been her only concern, it wouldn't have been a concern at all. She'd never had trouble finding another job. But she'd found things on the Lazy B that weren't so easily replaced—the big house she'd come to think of as home, the ability to look clear to forever and see nothing but land and sky, her friendships with Gun and with Colleen. Those were things not easily replaced.

Not to mention the heart she'd be leaving behind with Kel, she thought, her mouth twisting in a painful smile. Hearts weren't easy to replace, either, which was too bad, considering how badly broken hers was likely to end up.

She sighed. If she just had some idea how Kel felt about her. When they were in bed together, it was dangerously easy to tell herself that he couldn't make love to her with such passion and tenderness unless he loved her at least a little. But what Megan lacked in experience, she made up for in common sense. Kel was a skillful and considerate lover. There was no reason to think it was anything more than that.

And she'd looked for a reason, she thought. Her mouth curved in a sad smile. She wanted nothing more than to believe that there was something more to their relationship on Kel's part than a certain friendship and the fact that they were compatible in bed. But if there was, he was certainly keeping it close to his vest.

They'd all been sitting at the dinner table last week when Colleen—a much happier Colleen than the girl she'd first met, Megan thought with satisfaction—had read Gracie's letter aloud. And when she reached the part where Grace mentioned that she'd be staying with her daughter a little while longer, Megan's eyes had slid compulsively in Kel's direction. But if it had occurred to him that Gracie's return meant her own departure, the idea didn't seem to disturb him.

He hadn't, either then or in the days since, said anything about her staying on past the originally agreed-upon time. If she had any pride, she supposed she wouldn't have continued to spend her nights in his bed. But if memories were all she was going to have of him then she wanted to store up as many as possible.

Of course, with every day that passed, it was becoming more of a possibility that she was going to be taking something more substantial with her when she left. She touched her fingers lightly against her stomach, wondering if her mild symptoms were a result of wishful thinking. And wondering if she'd completely lost her mind that she should actually be hoping she was right.

But crazy or not, she was hoping. She couldn't have Kel, but if she could have his baby... Megan didn't have any romantic illusions about how difficult it would be to raise a child on her own. Her peripatetic life-style was fine for her, but she couldn't drag a baby all over the country with her. She'd have to try to find a stable job, which wouldn't be particularly easy to do while she was pregnant. And that was only the first and probably the least of the problems she'd have to deal with.

Before she even got to that point, there was the question of how Kel would feel about becoming a father. It wasn't a topic that had come up between them. They hadn't really talked about birth control, he'd simply provided it from the start, but the only completely foolproof method was abstention, and they certainly hadn't done that.

Megan plucked another green bean and bit into it absently. They'd talked of a lot of different things, but Kel's feelings on parenthood hadn't been among them. But she couldn't imagine that he would walk away from his own child. He had too much sense of responsibility for that.

But if a sense of responsibility was *all* he could give her child, it might be better if he was completely out of the picture. Megan knew from experience just how painful it was to know that you were a responsibility to someone and nothing more.

When her mother had dumped her on their doorstep, her grandparents had taken her in because they felt it was their responsibility to do so. Megan had sat silently in the chair she'd been given and listened to the discussion. If they didn't take her, she'd end up in foster care, an additional burden on an already overloaded system. There'd been no help for it—they'd have to raise her themselves.

There'd been a note of stern resignation in her grandfather's tone that had chilled Megan's childish heart. At six, she'd overheard her parents quarreling about which one of them *had* to take custody of her. Her mother had lost that battle and Megan had never seen her father again. Two years later, her mother had met a man who wanted to show her the world but not with an eight-year-old in tow. And it became obvious that her grandparents didn't really want her either.

It had taken Megan years to realize that there wasn't anything wrong with her, that it had simply been her misfortune to be born to parents too selfish to love anyone except themselves, and then to be handed over to an elderly couple whose last wish had been to start the arduous task of rearing a child all over again.

No child of hers was ever going to be made to feel like a burden, she thought, frowning at a butterfly that was drifting lazily between the rows of beans. If that was the best Kel could offer, then they'd manage without him.

The vehemence of the thought drew her up short. She didn't even know if there *was* a baby, for heaven's sake, let alone how Kel would react if there was. She bent and picked up the pan of beans and started to the house, her mouth twisted in a self-deprecating smile. Until she knew for sure that there was something to worry about, it was a little premature to try to guess how Kel would react, let alone get upset with him over it.

From the window of his office, Kel watched Megan walk down from the garden. She was wearing a pair of bright green shorts that exposed a tantalizing amount of leg, a red T-shirt that clung in all the right places and a ridiculous red baseball cap. She'd drawn her fair hair back in a ponytail, a practical style that somehow managed to look sexy and sassy on her. Battered white sneakers and bright yellow socks completed the outfit.

Kel felt his mouth curve upward. She reminded him of a brightly wrapped Christmas present, the kind that you wanted to unwrap first on Christmas morning. Megan disappeared behind the corner of the house, and a few seconds later he heard the thud of the kitchen screen door closing behind her.

His smile fading, he turned to his desk, but he didn't sit down again. There was a stack of paperwork sitting there, bills to be paid, records to be updated, letters to be answered. Kel ignored them all.

The house was quiet around him. Colleen had gone into town with Gun to get a part he'd ordered for that junk heap of a Vette. Since the two of them had patched up their differences, Colleen had become Gun's shadow, the way she had been before the accident. It was good to see his little sister happy again. That was something for which he owed Megan thanks.

Megan. With Colleen gone, there was nothing to stop him from going out to the kitchen, persuading her to drop whatever she was doing and taking her upstairs to spend an hour or two in bed. His body stirred in response to the thought, but Kel resisted the pull.

Among the papers on his desk was a letter from Gracie saying that she'd be returning to the Lazy B in two weeks, since her daughter was almost ready to manage without help. The letter had forced him to face an issue he'd been doing his best to dodge, namely, the fact that summer was creeping to an end and so was the time he and Megan had originally agreed upon for her to stay. When Gracie returned, Megan would go, it was that simple.

Unless he did something to stop her, she'd pack her things into her little blue car and drive out of his life. Unless he did something to stop her. The question was, did he want to stop her? And if so, why?

He spun away from the desk and stared out the window again. He knew the answer to the first question—he didn't want Megan to go, not now, not yet. As for why... What did it matter why, he thought irritably. He wanted her to stay because he liked having her in his bed. For that matter, he liked her companionship out of bed, too. She was intelligent and quick-witted. She made him laugh, and she'd helped put a smile on Colleen's face, something he hadn't been able to do in six months of trying.

He wanted her to stay because he did. That was reason enough.

But would she want to stay? She'd spent the last half dozen years or so traveling, obviously because she didn't choose to settle in one place. She might be more than ready to move on.

Besides, how could he suggest she stay on? Once Gracie returned, Megan's job would be gone. They didn't need two housekeepers, Colleen didn't need a paid companion and while Megan's riding skills had improved considerably, he could hardly offer her a job as a hand. So what was he going to say? Stay because we're good in bed together? Stay because I want you to?

"Damn." Kel muttered the curse under his breath.

He didn't want her to go but he didn't know how to ask her to stay.

* * *

"Word is, Kurt and Melissa Anderson are splitting up," Colleen said, sounding regretful.

"That's not much of a surprise." Kel reached for a second biscuit and pried it open before slathering it with butter. "Not when you consider the way they got married."

"You mean because Melissa got pregnant?"

Megan hadn't been paying much attention to the conversation until then but Colleen's comment brought her head up.

"Not the best way to start a marriage," Kel said, shrugging.

"Peggy Matheson thought she did it deliberately, to force Kurt to marry her," Colleen said, dabbing her fork in her mashed potatoes.

"If she did, she's probably regretting it now." That was Gun, reaching for the gravy bowl and pouring a generous amount over the thick slab of roast on his plate.

"I take it this was something of a shotgun marriage?" Megan asked, surprised by how steady her voice was. She even managed to sound mildly amused, as if the idea of a shotgun wedding this late in the twentieth century was a joke.

"Melissa's father would have made it one if Kurt hadn't asked her to marry him," Kel said.

"You're kidding." Though he hadn't sounded as if he was kidding.

"No." He looked at her, one brow lifted in an expression of mild surprise. "Melissa is Dave's only daughter, and he's pretty protective of her. And if

Dave hadn't been around, she's got four brothers who'd make sure Kurt lived up to his responsibilities.''

"Oh." Megan swallowed and looked at her plate.

Live up to his responsibilities? He'd sounded as if marriage had been a foregone conclusion, under the circumstances. Good lord, did that mean that Kel would feel the same if she really was carrying his baby? Would he feel obliged to marry her? The thought made her stomach knot with conflicting feelings. She loved him, of course she wanted to marry him, but not like that, not because he felt obligated to do so.

"Whatever the reason they got married, I think it's too bad that they're splitting up," Colleen said. "They seemed to love each other. Or at least, she loved him."

"Love isn't always enough," Kel said. "Especially not when it's one-sided."

"It's too bad there's a kid involved," Gun said, shaking his head. "They're always the ones that end up hurt the most when a family splits up."

"How old is he or she?" Megan asked, forcing the words past the lump in her throat.

"She must be five or so," Gun said, glancing at Kel for confirmation. Kel shrugged his lack of knowledge but Colleen nodded.

About the same age I was. She didn't realize she'd spoken the thought out loud until Colleen responded.

"You were five when your parents divorced? That must have been rough."

Annoyed with herself, Megan shrugged. "It wasn't as bad as it might have been. They weren't particularly happy together and they weren't the sort to suffer in silence." Her smile was ironic rather than bitter. She'd long since let go of that particular hurt.

"I thought you said your grandparents raised you," Kel said, his eyes curious. "I assumed your parents were dead."

"No. My mother got stuck with me after the divorce but when she decided to remarry a couple of years later, she deposited me with her parents. I haven't seen her since."

"How awful," Colleen exclaimed. Her green eyes flashed with anger on Megan's behalf. "How could she just leave you like that?"

"Apparently, it wasn't too difficult." Megan smiled to show that the scars of abandonment were long healed over. "She wasn't suited to being a mother. I can't say I felt any terrible regret at seeing the last of her."

"You were lucky you had your grandparents," Kel said slowly.

"Yes." She didn't elaborate. In a sense she *had* been lucky. At least she'd been fed and clothed. It was more than some children had. "From the sound of it, your friends' child won't have to worry about nobody wanting her," she said, turning the subject away from herself.

"No," Gun said. "Melissa and Kurt may not make it as a couple but they love that kid. It's probably what kept them together this long."

Megan was relieved when the conversation moved on to other topics. She didn't want to talk about her own childhood any more than she wanted to talk about the unknown Kurt and Melissa's impending separation. She nibbled at her food, her appetite gone. Her mind was spinning with this new insight into how Kel might react to finding out he was about to become a father.

Kel ran his hand through Megan's hair, enjoying the cool feel of it sifting through his fingers. She lay pressed along his side, molded to him from shoulder to hip, one leg nestled intimately between his, one hand splayed across his chest.

He liked the feel of her lying there, liked the feel of her in his bed. If she left, he'd miss these quiet moments as much as he missed the lovemaking that preceded them. He thought again of Gracie's letter lying downstairs on his desk. She'd be home next week.

He had to talk to Megan about what was going to happen when Gracie returned, about the possibility of staying on for a while. Maybe she could do some secretarial work for him. She must have worked in an office at some point, she seemed to have worked just about everywhere else. Or she could just stay on as a friend. Colleen had come to care about her and he . . . Well, he couldn't put a description to how he felt, but he didn't want her to go.

Megan threaded her fingers through the mat of dark hair on Kel's chest and tried not to wonder how many more nights she'd have like this one. She felt as if she'd been living in a dreamworld for the past three months, as if this summer had been a time apart from reality. But summer was coming to an end and reality lay just around the corner.

Or maybe it lay beneath her heart.

Somewhere deep inside, she knew that she was carrying Kel's child. She didn't need to see a little plastic stick turn pink or get a doctor's confirmation. She could sense a change in her body, a subtle shifting to accommodate the new life growing inside.

She had to make some decisions and she had to make them soon.

Kel let his hand drift down Meg's back, tracing the curve of her spine with one fingertip, feeling her shiver of response. After all these weeks, he was still surprised by how much he wanted her. It was a hunger that couldn't be appeased. It seemed to be the same for her.

Her hand shifted downward, her fingers brushing across his stirring arousal in a light, teasing caress that stole his breath. Kel brought his hand up, winding his fingers in his hair and tilting her head. He caught the glitter of her eyes in the moonlight and then his mouth closed over hers.

Tomorrow would be soon enough to make decisions, he thought. He'd talk with her tomorrow. For tonight, it was enough that she felt so incredibly right in his bed, in his arms.

Megan gave herself up to the hunger of Kel's mouth, arching her body to press herself against him as he leaned over her.

Tomorrow, she told herself. Tomorrow would be soon enough to make decisions. Tonight, she'd think of nothing but Kel and how right this felt.

Megan stuck her head around the edge of the door and looked at Kel. "You wanted to see me?"

"Come in." Kel stood up from behind the desk, disgusted to find himself as nervous as a kid about to go before the principal. "Shut the door."

Megan's brows arched. "Sounds ominous. Did I put too much salt in the stew last night?"

"The stew was fine." He forced a smile as he came around to sit on the corner of the desk. "I just wanted to talk to you for a minute. Have a seat."

Megan sank into the big leather chair in front of the desk and looked at him. He looked at her for a moment and then looked away. Whatever he had to say, he seemed to be having trouble finding the words he wanted.

She felt her stomach tighten uneasily. Kel was hardly the stereotype of the strong, silent cowboy. She'd never seen him at a loss for words before and she couldn't imagine why it should happen now. Unless he thought she was going to be upset by what he had to say.

"I got another letter from Gracie," he said abruptly. "She's coming home next week."

The knot in her stomach tightened painfully but Megan didn't let her expression so much as flicker. It wasn't as if it was a surprise. She'd known this was coming, known it would be soon.

"That's great," she said brightly. "Her daughter must be doing much better."

"I guess so." Kel was thrown off-balance by her quick enthusiasm. Didn't she realize what this meant? "You've...done a terrific job," he said, thinking how stupid the words sounded, even as he spoke. Next he was going to be offering her a bonus, for God's sake.

"I told you I'd make a good housekeeper," she said, reminding him of his initial reluctance to hire her.

"You were right." Was it his imagination or was her smile just a little too bright around the edges? As if, perhaps, she didn't want to leave? "Gracie's been gone a little longer than we expected," he said slowly.

"I know. I didn't expect the job to last as long as it has."

Kel's fingers tightened over the letter opener he'd been toying with. Did that mean that she was sorry it had lasted this long? Was she anxious to leave? Since she'd moved around so much, it was reasonable to assume that she felt the lure of new places, new people. What made him think she'd be interested in staying in one spot, especially when he wasn't offering any promises?

"I guess you're anxious to get on to the next place," he said slowly, watching her face for some sign of regret.

"Sure." Megan's face felt frozen and stiff but she forced a smile. "Always a new adventure."

"Must be fun."

"Oh, yes." She felt as if she was slowly bleeding to death inside.

"I suppose sticking in one place would seem pretty dull to you," he said, probing for some sign that she'd stay if he asked her, for some hint that she didn't want to go.

"Hmm." He could interpret that as agreement if he liked. She was afraid to open her mouth for fear she'd beg him to let her stay.

"Megan, I—" Whatever he'd been about to say was lost in the shrill ring of the phone. He hesitated, not wanting to interrupt his conversation with Megan.

"Go ahead and answer it," she said, apparently not sharing his desire to continue the discussion. "I have things to do." The phone rang again as she stood up.

"There are things we need to talk about," Kel said, feeling as if he was watching her slip through his fingers.

"It doesn't have to be this minute," she said lightly. "I'll be here another week."

She was already on her way to the door, and the phone shrilled a third time. Muttering a curse, Kel reached for it as she went out the door. She was right. He had another week.

Megan made her way up the stairs, feeling her knees threaten to buckle with each step. But they supported her long enough for her to reach her room. She closed the door behind her and leaned against it, closing her eyes.

She'd known this was coming, of course. It wasn't as if the news that Grace Cavenaugh was returning was unexpected. She had, as Kel said, been gone longer than she'd intended as it was. But apparently expecting something was not enough to take away the pain of dealing with it when it happened.

I'm pregnant. Two little words was all she had to say and there'd be no question of her leaving. Kel would live up to his responsibilities the same way his friend Kurt had done. He'd want to marry her and she might be weak enough to give in to the temptation.

They'd get married. And a few years from now, people would be discussing the breakup of their marriage, the same way they'd discussed Kurt and Melissa Anderson's a couple of nights ago. And there'd be another child caught up in the middle of a divorce, the same way she had been.

Not that it would be the same, because *her* child would certainly never be less than wanted. But even under the best of circumstances, a divorce was difficult for all involved, especially a child. And what about her feelings? Could she stand to live with Kel, knowing he'd only married her because she was pregnant, knowing he didn't love her?

But he might come to love you.

Megan's soft laugh held an edge of hysteria. When would she ever learn? She'd spent years thinking that her grandparents would come to love her. If only she was a good girl and didn't make them angry, they'd love her eventually. All those years of being a good little girl hadn't been enough. And being a good little wife to Kel wouldn't be enough, either.

She pushed herself away from the door and went to the closet. Pulling her suitcase off the top shelf, she set it on the bed and opened it, the sound of the zipper harsh in the quiet room.

She wasn't going to let herself fall into that pattern again. She'd spent years trying to please other people, trying to make herself into someone they could love. And if she'd learned nothing else from those years, it was that you couldn't make yourself lovable to another person. They either loved you or they didn't.

If she stayed, if she told Kel about the baby, he would marry her. And she'd find herself falling into the old patterns, smiling when she didn't want to smile, pretending to be happy when she wasn't. And eventually, she'd end up hating herself and maybe hating Kel a little, too, because he couldn't love her the way she needed to be loved. They both deserved better than that. And even more important, their child deserved better.

She heard the front door close and left her room and went across the hall to Kel's room, hurrying to the window. He was striding across the yard to the barn, the long, rolling stride of someone who spent a lot of hours in the saddle. He disappeared into the barn but she stayed where she was, watching. A few minutes later, he led Dude out and swung into the saddle.

He seemed to hesitate a moment, looking toward the house. Megan flattened herself against the wall beside the window, though she doubted he could see her at that distance anyway. After a bit, Kel tightened his hands on the reins and nudged the big horse with his heel, turning him out of the ranch yard.

Megan watched until he was out of sight, not troubling to conceal the hunger in her eyes. This was the last glimpse she'd have of him. Kel disappeared around the curve of a hill, and she closed her eyes against the pain in her chest.

You could stay.

She tried to ignore the small, weak voice, the one that said being with Kel was worth any price. Only it wasn't. It wasn't worth her self-respect.

It seemed to take an enormous amount of effort to push herself away from the wall and go to her room. It shouldn't take long to finish packing. She couldn't bear to wait another week. It would hurt too much. Now that she knew her time here was ending, she wanted to sever the ties as quickly as possible.

Colleen was with the physical therapist so there was no one to question her leaving. Megan hesitated, thinking of Colleen. It wasn't only Kel she was going to miss. She and Colleen had developed a real friendship these past few weeks. She hoped the girl wouldn't be too hurt when she found out Megan had left without a word. But there was no help for it.

For a moment, Megan almost gave in to despair. She was leaving so much behind. The pain of it was almost more than she could bear. But she was taking a great deal with her, she thought, pressing her hand to her still flat stomach. The thought gave her the strength to finish packing.

Years of travel had pared her belongings down to the bare minimum. Less than an hour after leaving Kel's study, Megan was tiptoeing down the stairs. She set her suitcase down in the entryway and went into Kel's study to set the note she'd written on his desk. She'd spent more time writing the note than she had packing, and she still wasn't satisfied with the result, but she'd finally decided it would have to do. Since she couldn't tell the truth, there really was no intelligent explanation for her abrupt departure.

Megan lingered a moment in the study. This was where he'd kissed her the first time, where he'd told her that, if she stayed, they were going to become lovers. She'd thought then that she should run, that she was going to end up with a broken heart if she stayed. And she'd been right, she thought ruefully. But she wasn't sorry she'd stayed. The child she carried was a gift of love, even if it was only her own love for Kel.

A few minutes later, she turned the nose of her bright blue compact out of the ranch yard and pointed it toward the highway. In less than a minute, a curve in the road hid the ranch house from her when she looked in the rearview mirror. Blinking back tears, she tried not to think about how much she'd left behind.

Chapter 10

Spring, Three Years Later

Kel slowed the rental car at the intersection and checked the street sign against the slip of paper in his hand. The names matched, which meant he should turn left. He made the turn and then pulled over to the curb and let the car idle. Hands resting on the steering wheel, he stared out the windshield at the tidy residential street in front of him.

It was a nice neighborhood, high-priced for Cheyenne. The houses were large, as were the trees that lined the street. The lawns were green with early spring growth, and there were a few early flowers to add a touch of color here and there. Nothing in the charming picture accounted for the grim expression on Kel's face. He reached into the pocket of his denim jacket and pulled out the envelope there. He stared at it but he didn't bother drawing out the letter it contained. He had the few sentences memorized.

> Dear Kel,
>
>   I need to speak to you. I would prefer to do so in person but unfortunately, I am unable to make the trip north at this time. Is there any chance that you'll be in the Cheyenne area anytime in the near future?
>
>   Please forgive the mystery. It's just that things will be so much easier to explain face-to-face.

She'd given an address and a phone number and signed herself, "Sincerely yours, Megan Roarke."

Sincerely his. Not likely.

Kel's fingers tightened around the envelope, crumpling it. The only thing more surprising than Megan's letter was finding himself here, responding to her request to see him. After the way she'd disappeared three years ago, his first impulse had been to throw the letter in the trash and forget about her. Again.

But if he was honest, he had to admit he hadn't done as good a job as he might have wished of forgetting her the first time around. Not if all it took was the sight of her name on the bottom of an impersonal note to bring her image sharply to mind. The hurt she'd dealt him when she left so abruptly was more tender than he would have liked.

All the more reason to ignore her now, he thought. Whatever she had to say, he wasn't interested. She'd told him everything that mattered when she'd walked out. Not that she'd been obligated to do more, he admitted grudgingly.

There'd been no promises, overt or implied, between them. It wasn't Megan's fault that he'd been halfway to falling in love with her and had only just realized it when she disappeared. Really, he supposed he should be grateful that she'd gone when she did. Otherwise, he'd probably have made a damn fool of himself.

Kel drummed his fingers on the steering wheel. He'd let the letter sit on his desk for close to a week, eyeing it as if it offered some physical danger. Several times he'd started to throw it away, and each time he'd changed his mind. Now, he half wished he'd thrown it out after all. If he had, he wouldn't be sitting here like a nervous boy about to pick up his first date.

Damn Megan Roarke anyway. Kel thumped his fist on the steering wheel. Three years ago, she'd persuaded him to hire her, then made herself so damned irresistible that he'd not only taken her into his bed, he'd let her halfway into his heart, and then she'd disappeared. Now, here she was, popping back into his life.

He could always turn the car around and leave. He didn't owe her anything. But he had to admit that his curiosity was aroused. *Things will be so much easier to explain face-to-face,* her letter said. What things? What could she possibly have to say to him after all this time?

With a sigh, he pulled away from the curb. Whatever she wanted, she could say it and get it over with and then he could go home and forget her. Again.

The address she'd given him proved to be a small house tucked slightly to the rear of a larger home. Kel parked and got out, grateful to be free of the rental car's too small interior. He felt as if he'd had his knees up next to his ears. Centuries from now, when archaeologists traced the history of the automobile, they were sure to conclude that, in the late twentieth century, Americans suddenly developed much shorter legs, he thought, shutting the car door with a disgusted swing of his hand.

Thinking of legs made him remember Megan's legs, ridiculously long legs for such a small woman. And he had a ridiculously clear image of them, considering he'd all but forgotten her.

"Damn." Kel muttered the word under his breath as he circled the car and started down the gravel driveway to the house. He wished more than ever that he hadn't let his curiosity drive him to respond to Megan's letter. She'd been out of his life, out of his thoughts, and that's where he'd like her to stay.

The heels of his boots sounded loud on the wooden steps of the porch. It was the middle of the afternoon on a weekday, and he assumed that most of the surrounding houses were empty, their owners at work. Now that he thought about it, it seemed odd that Megan would be home this time of day. Was she between jobs? Or maybe she was so anxious to talk to him that she'd taken a day off? He hadn't really provided many options, he thought. During their brief, stilted phone conversation, he'd pretty much given her a time and day and let his tone imply that she could take it or leave it. His conscience gave an uneasy twinge and was ignored. She'd been the one to ask to see him, not the other way around. If this wasn't a convenient time for her, tough.

Ignoring the doorbell, Kel tugged open the screen door and rapped his knuckles on the solid wooden door. He let the screen door close and waited. A moment later, he heard movement inside the house. He was annoyed to feel his heart immediately begin to beat a little faster. He deliberately turned away and forced himself to admire the beautiful new spring growth on the maple tree that grew between this house and the larger one to the east.

He heard the door open but took his time turning to face the woman who'd haunted far more of his dreams than he'd willingly admit. His first thought was that she hadn't changed at all. Her hair was still the same pale gold he remembered, her eyes were just as big and beautiful and her mouth... God, her mouth made him think of things he'd done his damnedest to forget.

His second thought was that he wanted her just as much as he ever had. It had been like this from the first time he saw her—one look and he'd wanted her so much it had been hard to think clearly. The realization angered him, put an edge to his voice.

"Megan."

"Hello, Kel."

Just the sound of her saying his name brought a rush of memories with it. Sometimes, when they'd been making love, she'd say his name on a husky little moan as if it had been wrung from deep inside her. Damn her! One look and the old hunger was back, as strong as ever.

"Are we going to have our conversation standing on the porch?" he asked, lacing the question with more sarcasm than it warranted. He wanted to hear whatever she had to say, tell her no to any favors she might want to ask and get out of here.

"Sorry." He thought she flushed though it was difficult to tell with the screen still between them. "Please, come in."

The house was as small as it had looked from the outside, but she'd decorated the rooms so that the word that came to mind was cozy rather than cramped. The living room held a small sofa, covered with floral print in shades of blue and that purply-pink women called mauve. Stupid name for a color, Kel thought as he stopped next to it. The rest of the room picked up the colors of the sofa in a mixture of solids and stripes that should have looked cluttered and irritating and managed to look friendly and soothing instead.

Too bad he wasn't in the mood to be soothed, Kel thought sourly. Nor was he feeling particularly friendly. He heard Megan shut the front door and turned to look at her. But his irritated suggestion that they cut the polite preliminaries and get to whatever it was she wanted to say died unspoken. The screen had blurred her image more than he'd realized. Seeing her without its protection, he momentarily forgot his irritation.

Megan had never been what he would have called robust-looking, but the woman who stood in front of him looked as if a strong wind would knock her over. She'd lost weight, a lot of it. She was wearing a soft pink blouse and a full skirt in a darker shade of the same color. Neither garment concealed the almost painful thinness of the body beneath. Her cheekbones stood out beneath a layer of skin so pale it looked almost translucent. Her eyes were the same blue-gray he remembered, but there were blue shadows beneath them that hadn't been there before. And her hair, while it was the same pale gold, was dull and tired-looking, the life drained from it.

Either Megan knew how drastically her appearance had changed or his expression gave away his thoughts. She lifted her hand to touch her hair.

"I know I look like I just got off the wreck of the Hesperus," she said with a self-conscious laugh. "I had a touch of pneumonia."

"Are you over it?"

"Oh, yes. I'm fine."

She didn't look fine, he thought, noticing the hand she'd set on the back of a wing chair as if she needed it to steady herself.

"I'm glad you're better" was all he said.

"Not as glad as I am," she said, smiling. "Can I get you something to drink?"

"No, thanks."

There was a stilted moment of silence and then Megan gestured to the sofa. "Why don't you have a seat?"

He started to refuse but then it occurred to him that she probably wouldn't sit down unless he did, and from the looks of her, he doubted she was up to standing for any length of time. Irritated with himself for being concerned about her health, he sat on the edge of the sofa. Megan chose the wing chair. Their eyes met for a moment and they both looked away.

"Nice place," Kel said and then could have kicked himself for coming up with such a banal comment.

"Thank you. It was built for the former owner's mother to live in. I rent it from the man who owns the property now. He lives in the big house." She nodded in the direction of the house to the east, one corner of it just visible out the multipaned front window. "He's a lawyer and I've worked for him the last couple of years so it's worked out quite well."

"Mmm." Kel made a noncommittal sound. He didn't give a damn about her living arrangements or who she worked for. He just wanted to know why he was here.

There was another of those awkward little pauses and this time it was Megan who broke it. "How's Colleen?"

"She's fine. She's going to school in Fort Collins."

"How's her leg? Did it heal all right?"

"Pretty much. She only limps if she pushes too hard and gets really tired." What the hell did she care how Colleen's leg was? She'd walked out on his little sister the same time she'd walked out on him. Kel felt his anger, which had been momentarily softened by the lingering evidence of her illness, stir again.

"And Gun? How's Gun?"

"Fine. He's working for a friend of mine in Colorado, Conner Fox."

"Is Zeke still terrorizing the hands?"

"He'll outlast most of us."

"Probably." Megan's mouth curved in a soft smile that held more than a trace of nostalgia, and Kel felt his patience give out.

"Look, you didn't write me because you had the urge to discuss old acquaintances," he said, not troubling to hide his irritation. "You said you had something to tell me and that you wanted to say it face-to-face. What is it?"

What little color there'd been in her face drained away, but Kel refused to feel guilty. Whatever she had to say, she could spit it out. He had no intention of sitting here pretending that they were old friends.

"I appreciate your coming to see me," she said, after a moment. "I know it must have seemed odd, my writing after all this time."

"We haven't exactly maintained a regular correspondence," Kel said with dry sarcasm.

"I must have sounded mysterious." She smoothed her skirt over her knee with fingers that trembled slightly. "I suppose I could have told you in a letter," she said, almost as if speaking to herself. "But I couldn't find the right words and—"

"Tell me what?" he interrupted impatiently. He wasn't in the mood for whatever game she was playing.

She didn't say anything for a moment and then she sighed. "I can't find the words now, either," she muttered. "Maybe showing you is the best way, after all."

"Show me what?"

Rather than answer with words, Megan turned and pulled open a drawer in the pine table beside her chair.

Reaching in, she drew out a framed photograph. She set the photo in her lap and then shut the drawer very carefully, as if it was important to shut it just so. Then she picked up the photo and looked at it for a long moment.

Kel stirred restlessly. He wanted out of here, out of this cozy little room, away from the soft floral scent of her perfume, away from the sight of her. Seeing her stirred up too many memories.

"For God's sake, Megan," he snapped when she continued to sit there without moving. "Just cut the bull and tell me whatever it is you wanted to tell me."

By way of answer, she held the picture out to him, her hand shaking so badly, it was a wonder she didn't drop it. Kel took it from her, throwing her an irritated glance before looking down at the photo. He didn't know what the hell kind of game she was playing, but whatever it was, he—

He felt his heart stop for an instant and then start beating with slow, heavy thuds. It was a studio portrait, with the usual vaguely sky blue background. The subject was standing in the center, both hands planted on his hips as he stared at the camera with a challenging look out of all proportion to his size and age.

Though Kel had never seen the child in the photograph before, he knew the face well. He'd seen it in old family pictures often enough. The mop of thick dark hair that held hints of red, the solid chin, the green eyes. The toddler in the photo was the spitting image of himself at the same age.

He felt as if he'd just been thrown from a very tall horse and had all the wind knocked out of him by the impact. He had to swallow twice before he could find a voice, and the one he found was hoarse and unfamiliar, like listening to someone else speak.

"Who is he?"

There was a heartbeat's pause and then Megan's whispered response.

"His name is Michael. He's your son."

Megan saw the impact of her words strike Kel with the force of a physical blow. He actually jerked in his seat.

"My son." The words were neither question nor statement.

"He...he was born in March." She couldn't bear to let the silence stretch. "He's two now but people usually think he's older because he's so big for his age. The doctor thinks he's going to be tall." She knew she was babbling but she couldn't seem to stop. "I guess he gets that from his—"

"Did you know?" Kel's hoarse voice cut through her chatter without apology. "When you left, did you know you were pregnant?"

Megan slumped back in her chair as a wave of relief swept over her. She hadn't realized until that moment how tense she'd been, afraid that Kel might doubt Michael's paternity.

"I...suspected," she said quietly.

"You suspected." His fingers tightened over the picture frame until the knuckles shone white with strain. "Why didn't you say something?"

"I wasn't sure I was pregnant and I—"

"What about when you were sure?" He lifted his eyes from the photograph, and Megan felt a tremor of fear at the rage she saw there. "There must have come a time when you didn't have any more doubts about it," he said, his voice silky. "Maybe when you were in labor? Or when the doctor handed you the baby? You couldn't possibly have had much doubt then. Didn't it occur to you that I might like to know I was a father? That I might like to know I had a son?"

When she didn't answer but only continued to sit there staring at him with those big eyes, Kel felt his rage edge upward to the point where, for a split second, he actually wanted to strike her. He shot to his feet, aware that the sudden movement made Megan start, as if she'd sensed that he teetered on the edge of violence and was afraid of him.

Good, he thought savagely. She *should* be afraid of him. She should be scared to death of him. After what she'd done, it was the least she owed him. She'd kept his child from him. His fingers tightened around the picture frame. His son was two years old. Spinning away from Megan, he strode to the window, wanting to put as much distance between them as possible, which wasn't nearly enough in such a small room.

Staring at the picture, he tried to absorb the reality of what she'd told him. He had a child. A son. He was two years old and his name was Michael and he was big for his age. And Kel didn't know another damned thing about him.

"Why?" The single word was all he could force through the tightness in his throat.

"I don't know."

"You don't know?" Megan flinched from the contempt in his eyes. "You keep my son from me and all you can say is you don't know?"

"At first I wasn't absolutely sure and then when I was, it seemed—" She lifted her hands in a confused gesture before letting them fall to her lap. "It just seemed too late," she finished weakly.

"Too late."

Megan flushed at Kel's contemptuous repetition of the phrase. Maybe it didn't make much sense now, but at the time, that was how it had felt. It had seemed as if all the bridges had been burned behind her, leaving her no choice but to continue on and try not to look back.

"What made you change your mind? Why are you telling me about . . . Michael now?"

"I began to think that maybe I hadn't been fair," she said, choosing her words carefully.

"It took three years for that to occur to you? I've missed out on the first two years of my son's life and it just now occurs to you that it wasn't fair?"

The pain she heard beneath the anger silenced Megan as nothing else could have done. She lowered her eyes from the stark hurt in his eyes and stared at her hands.

"I'm sorry." It was a wholly inadequate offering and Kel let her know as much.

"You're sorry?" he repeated incredulously. "You keep my own child from me for two years for no reason at all and all you can say is you're *sorry?*"

She lifted one shoulder to indicate it was the best she could do and heard Kel's mutter of disgust. He turned his back on her as if he couldn't trust himself if he had to look at her. Megan was surprised when that simple gesture made her eyes burn with tears.

She'd expected him to be angry. How could he be anything else? But she hadn't expected it to hurt so much. After almost three years, after the way he'd dismissed her from his life, she'd almost convinced herself that any feelings she had for Kel Bryan were based solely on the fact that he was the father of her child. Michael created a certain bond between them, even if Kel didn't know he existed.

Megan had been braced for the shock of seeing Kel again. But what she hadn't been prepared for was the almost overwhelming impact he had on her senses. She'd had to cling to the door to keep herself upright when she'd seen him standing on her porch.

As the months passed, she'd deliberately blocked his image from her mind, pushed it from her heart. It hadn't been easy at first, but when Michael was born, he'd absorbed every fiber of her time and attention, and his father's image had finally begun to grow a little shadowy. Megan had welcomed the change.

But one look at Kel and all the memories had come rushing back to her. It seemed as if every moment of those months she'd spent on his ranch were embedded so deeply in her mind that nothing could ever erase them. How could she have thought to forget how tall he was and the way his wide shoulders seemed to fill a doorway? The wavy darkness of his hair was the same as she remembered, a little shorter, maybe, as if he'd just gotten a haircut. She curled her fingers into her palm against the urge to touch his hair, to stroke the thick brush of a mustache that covered his upper lip, to smooth the lines beside his green eyes.

She'd been lying to herself all these months. She hadn't stopped loving Kel. She wondered despairingly if she ever would.

"Where is he?"

Megan had been so absorbed in her thoughts that it took her a moment to realize Kel had spoken. "What?"

"Where is he?"

"With my landlord." She didn't pretend not to know who he meant. "Reed knew you were coming today and he offered to take care of Michael for me."

"I want to see him."

It was no more than she'd expected, of course, but something in the flat demand sent a chill up her spine. "I don't want him upset."

"I'm not going to pounce on him," Kel said. He turned from the window to look at her, his eyes impatient. "Why did you tell me about him if you didn't expect me to want to see him?"

"Of course I expected you to want to see him. I just don't want you to upset him."

"I won't." When she still hesitated, his mouth tightened with irritation. "Since I assume he's next door, I can go get him myself, if you'd rather."

"No. I'll call Reed." She stood up, smoothing her hands over her skirt and drawing in a deep, calming breath before she went to the phone, which sat on a table near the sofa.

Kel noticed that Megan's fingers were shaking so badly that she was having trouble punching the right buttons on the phone. He couldn't find it in him to feel sorry. Not right now, not when he'd just learned that she'd cheated him out of the first two years of his son's life. The conversation was brief. She set the receiver down and turned toward him.

"Reed's bringing him over. It's almost time for his nap. He . . . might be a little cranky."

"Are you afraid I'll slug him if he cries?" He lifted one brow in question.

"No. No, of course not." She linked her fingers together in front of her. "I guess I just want you to see him on his best behavior," she said, giving him a quick, nervous smile. "Most parents feel that way, I think."

"I haven't had a chance to find that out," he said coldly. He bent to set the photo down. When he straightened, he looked at her with eyes as cold as his voice. "I'm not a recruiter for an exclusive nursery school, looking to be impressed, Megan. I'm his father."

"I know."

"Odd that it took you two years to figure that out."

Before she could say anything—and what could she have said?—Kel heard the squeak of the screen door, and then the front door was pushed open. He barely noticed the man who entered. His attention was all for the child balanced comfortably on his hip.

Michael.

His son.

Chapter 11

"Mama." Michael held out his arms when he saw Megan and she went to him immediately.

"Hello, muffin." She took him in her arms, her eyes meeting Reed's as she did so. She read the concern in his and forced a shaky smile to let him know that she was all right, though she wasn't sure of the truth of that right now.

With Michael in her arms, she turned to face Kel. And felt her heart nearly stop at the hunger in his eyes. It hit her suddenly that if she'd set out to do so, she could have found no more effective way to hurt Kel than to keep his child from him. That wasn't why she'd done it, but she doubted he'd ever believe that.

As soon as Michael saw Kel, he went still, his wide green eyes uncertain. Megan had to clear her throat before she could speak.

"Michael, this is Kel. He's your...your father."

"Hello, Michael," Kel said, his voice suspiciously gruff.

Michael stared at the big stranger a moment longer. At two, the word *father* had no particular meaning for him. But his mother's visitor was large and dark and unknown. With a quick jerk, he turned his face into Megan's shoulder, his small arms clinging to her as if expecting to be wrenched away at any moment.

Kel's expression froze but not before Megan caught the quick flicker of hurt in his eyes. She rubbed her son's small back, struggling to keep the tension she felt from transferring itself to him.

"He's a little shy," she said to Kel. "It's just that he doesn't know you yet."

"Who's fault is that?" Kel asked coldly.

"Depends on who's assigning the blame, I'd think," Reed said, his deep voice holding traces of a Southern drawl.

Kel had almost forgotten the other man's presence. Now, his eyes cut from Megan to her landlord and employer. And what else? he wondered.

"Kel, this is Reed Hall. Reed, this is Kel Bryan." Megan made perfunctory introductions.

Neither man offered to shake hands as they took stock of each other. When Megan had said that she rented the house from the lawyer she worked for and then had told him that Reed was taking care of Michael for her, Kel had vaguely imagined a balding, elderly gentleman, a grandfatherly type. But there was nothing grandfatherly about Reed Hall.

He was probably not much over forty, and from the looks of his lean body, a very in-shape forty. With his white-blond hair and pale green eyes, Kel guessed most women would find him attractive. And from the easy way he'd walked into the house, he was obviously quite at home here. Was he Megan's lover as well as employer, landlord and occasional baby-sitter? The possibility did nothing to endear Reed to him.

"I don't think this discussion concerns you," Kel said bluntly, responding to Reed's comment about who might be at fault.

"Megan's a friend of mine." Reed took a step forward so that he stood next to Megan. Protectively near her, Kel noticed with irritation.

"Reed."

Megan set her hand on his arm, but Kel missed whatever it was she said. For a moment, it seemed to Kel that he was looking at a family. Mother, father, child. Just the way it should be. Only the child just happened to be his, not Reed Hall's.

"The discussion still doesn't concern you," Kel said.

Reed started to say something but Megan forestalled him. "Could you put Michael down for his nap?" He hesitated, looking from her to Kel. "Please." She emphasized the word by tightening her fingers on his arm. "Please, Reed."

"Sure. Come here, champ. It's nap time for you." Michael clung to his mother.

"It's okay, Michael. Go with Uncle Reed," Megan told him.

He held on a moment longer before allowing Reed to peel him away. Kel caught the uneasy glance the boy threw in his direction and wondered if it was just that he felt shy around strangers or if Michael sensed the tensions in the room and had decided to place the blame squarely at Kel's feet.

A not entirely unjustified opinion, Kel thought. And watching another man carry his son away did nothing to improve his mood. Reed Hall held the boy with the ease of familiarity, a familiarity Kel bitterly resented. He watched until the two of them disappeared through a doorway that led to the rear of the house and then turned his gaze to Megan.

His eyes were ice green and just about as warm, Megan thought. She resisted the urge to shiver and set her hand on the back of the wing chair. She was still so darned weak from the pneumonia.

"*Uncle* Reed?" he sneered. "Is that the term for it these days?"

Megan flushed beneath the accusation in his eyes but she refused to look away. "Reed has been a very good friend to both of us," she said steadily.

"I'll just bet he has," Kel muttered.

Megan didn't respond. She wasn't going to defend her relationship with Reed, not to Kel, not to anyone. She wondered if Reed had been right. Maybe it had been a mistake to write to Kel. At least she could have waited until she was feeling a little stronger.

Of course, it was the pneumonia and the lingering weakness that followed it that had made her decide to contact him in the first place. It had suddenly struck her that if something happened to her, Michael would be left alone. If she'd waited until she was stronger, she might have talked herself out of writing to Kel, and no matter how difficult this was for her, she knew it was what was best for her son.

"All right, I want him," Kel said abruptly.

"Wh-what?" Megan felt as if she'd just been kicked in the chest. "What do you mean, you want him?"

"That's why you contacted me, isn't it? Because you figured I'd want the boy? Well, I do. I assume I'm listed on his birth certificate?"

Dazed, Megan nodded. She seemed to have lost track of the conversation somewhere. Kel thought she wanted him to take Michael?

"Then there shouldn't be any problem with my getting custody," he said briskly. "There'll be a lot of paperwork but—"

"There won't be any paperwork." She heard the shrillness in her voice but made no effort to lower it. "Why would you think I wanted you to take him?"

"Because you've discovered that being a single mother isn't easy. Maybe *Uncle* Reed doesn't mind being an uncle but he objects to being a daddy." Kel shrugged his indifference to her reasons. "I don't really care why. I just want to be sure the transition is as easy for him as possible."

"There's not going to be any transition." Megan's hand was trembling as she lifted it to her head. She wanted to sound forceful but she couldn't seem to catch her breath. Damn this weakness. Her voice sounded more shaken than commanding. "I'm not giving you custody of my son."

"My son, too," he reminded her in a silky voice. "Fathers have rights these days, especially in court."

"In court?" Megan stared at him. She was suddenly light-headed, and it seemed as if the floor was rocking under her.

"Megan?" Kel's voice was sharp. She looked white as a sheet, he thought. Abruptly, he remembered what she'd said about having been ill. She swayed and he took a quick step toward her. "Are you okay?"

"I'm fine," she said weakly and promptly fainted.

Kel caught her before she hit the floor, lifting her in his arms as easily as if she were a child. Not that she weighed much more than a child, he thought, shocked by the fragile feel of her in his arms.

He held her against his chest for a moment, staring into her face. With her eyes closed, the signs of illness were even easier to read, the hollows under her cheekbones, the blue shadows around her eyes. She must have been very sick. Had she come close to dying? There was a tight, hard knot in his chest at the thought. All the times he'd thought of Megan, he'd never considered the possibility of her death. And he didn't like considering it now.

Shaking his head, he carried her over to the small sofa and laid her down, tucking a throw pillow under her head for support. Her arm dangled off the side of the sofa and he picked it up and laid it across her stomach. It made her look distressingly like a corpse. Cursing under his breath, Kel crouched beside the sofa and took her hand in his, patting it gently. It seemed as if, in movies, they always patted somebody's hand if they fainted. Or dashed water in their face. He decided to start with the patting.

Maybe he'd been too hard on her, he thought, watching her face. He'd been so angry, he hadn't even tried to soften his words. But it had seemed like a reasonable assumption, he thought defensively. If she didn't want him to take the boy, why had she written to him at all? Despite the popular myths of motherhood, it wasn't as if women didn't change their minds about wanting children all the time. His mother had walked out on him and Colleen. If he remembered rightly, Megan's mother hadn't wanted her. Hell, that made it practically a tradition on both sides of the family, he thought with black humor.

"What happened?" Reed's sharp question made Kel glance over his shoulder before rising to his feet. "What did you do?"

"I didn't punch her, if that's what you think. She fainted."

Kel backed away to allow Reed next to Megan, annoyed at his reluctance to do so. He watched as Reed checked her pulse and put the back of his hand against her cheek. Kel had to curl his fingers into his palms against the urge to jerk the other man away from her.

"I suppose you had nothing to do with it?" Reed asked with heavy sarcasm. He straightened and faced Kel, his pale green eyes full of dislike. "What did you say to her?"

"I told her I'd take the boy off her hands," Kel said, curious to see Reed's reaction.

"You really are a prize bastard," Reed said after a moment, his drawl thickening a little. "I told her she was making a big mistake in contacting you. But she was so damned scared that something would happen to Michael that she wouldn't listen.''

"What do you mean? What could happen to Michael?"

Reed hesitated a moment, looking at Megan as if debating whether to answer the question. When he spoke, it was to ask a question.

"Did Megan tell you she'd been ill?"

"She said she'd had pneumonia," Kel admitted.

"She almost died," Reed said, confirming Kel's suspicions. "When she recovered, she started thinking about what would happen to Michael if something had happened to her. About him being left alone. She decided it would be better for him if you knew."

Kel winced a little when he thought of his assumption that Megan was tired of motherhood, but knowing her motivation didn't change his determination to be a part of his son's life.

Before he could respond to what Reed had told him, Megan stirred. She opened her eyes and stared at the two of them. With a soft exclamation, she immediately tried to sit up. Ignoring Reed's move forward, Kel bent over her and slid his arm under her shoulders to ease her into a sitting position. He was struck again by how incredibly fragile she seemed.

"How are you?" he asked quietly.

"I'm fine." She pushed her hair from her face and gave him an uncertain look. "I'm sorry."

"*You* don't need to apologize," Reed said with a pointed glance in Kel's direction.

"Reed," Megan said repressively. She turned worried eyes in Kel's direction. "We need to talk."

"You should rest," Reed protested.

"I can come back tomorrow," Kel said slowly. Much as he hated to find himself in agreement with Reed Hall, Megan didn't look up to the kind of discussion they needed to have.

"I'm fine." She moved as if to stand up and then apparently thought better of it and settled back onto the sofa. "I'm fine," she insisted, as if to convince herself as much as anyone.

"You should rest," Kel told her. "We can talk later."

"No. Please, Kel. I'm really fine." Reed snorted his opinion of that claim and she threw him a quick glance before looking at Kel. "Maybe if you could get me a glass of water?" she asked.

Kel didn't have to be a mind reader to know that she was worried about his implication that he'd take her to court over Michael. He hesitated, but he could hardly offer her reassurance when he was still reeling from the impact of finding out that he had a son.

"The kitchen's through there," Megan prompted, pointing.

She could have asked Reed to play water boy but she probably wanted a moment alone with him. The thought eliminated Kel's urge to insist that they postpone their discussion until Megan was feeling stronger. He turned and went in the direction she'd indicated.

The kitchen was as small as the rest of the house, but sunshine poured in through the window over the sink, brightening the room and making it look bigger than it was. Moving on automatic, Kel opened cupboard doors until he found the glasses. He moved to the sink and turned on the tap. But glancing out the softly curtained window, he found himself looking at a miniature playground, constructed of brightly colored plastic modules. There was a tiny slide and arches to crawl through and places for just sitting and contemplating the joys of being a child.

He didn't question the instinct that told him the child-size play area had been furnished courtesy of Reed Hall. The thought hurt more than it had any business doing. So what if another man had bought Michael a fancy jungle gym? And acted as a father to him?

Forgotten, the water continued to run while Kel stared out the window and contemplated the idea that another man had been a surrogate father to his son. His son. No matter how many times he thought the words, they didn't seem real. Yet nothing could be more real than the gut-level sense of recognition he'd felt when he saw the boy. It almost seemed as though, if he'd seen Michael under other circumstances, he'd still have known the boy was his son. It was something deeper than the obvious physical resemblance between them.

The sound of the front door closing snapped Kel out of his thoughts. He became aware of the water still running in the sink and the empty glass in his hand. He filled it and shut the tap off but stayed where he was a moment longer. He had no idea what he was going to say to Megan. What she'd done was unforgivable. She'd cost him the first two years of Michael's life, time he could never regain. It had seemed best, she'd said. How could it be best for anyone to keep him apart from his son? Obviously, he wasn't going to find any answers standing here, he thought.

Megan was sitting in the same place, and Kel was relieved to see that there seemed to be a little more color in her cheeks. She took the glass from him and swallowed thirstily.

"Thank you."

"Where's your friend?" he asked, glancing around as if expecting to find Reed concealed behind the curtains.

"Reed went back to his house." Megan set the glass down on the end table.

"I'm surprised he was willing to leave you at my mercy."

"He wasn't crazy about the idea," Megan admitted with a small smile. "But I convinced him you wouldn't do me any bodily harm."

He questioned her confidence with an arched brow but didn't say anything.

"Would you mind sitting down?" She indicated the wing chair. "I'm getting a crick in my neck looking up at you."

He sat down. And the silence suddenly stretched between them like a living thing. There was so much to be said, so many questions to be asked, answers to be given.

"I'm sorry, Kel. I know that seems pretty inadequate right now but it's the best I can offer."

"What's done is done," he said, abruptly weary. "You can't give me back the two years I've lost."

"No." Megan looked at her hands where they lay clasped in her lap. "You didn't mean it, did you? About taking me to court over Michael?" There was a small tremor in her voice that betrayed her attempt at calm.

Kel was silent so long that Megan thought he was going to ignore her question. "I don't know," he said finally.

"I'd fight you, and Michael would end up caught in the middle." She lifted her eyes to his face, willing to beg, if necessary. Where her son was concerned, pride was irrelevant. "He's not much more than a baby, Kel. He needs his mother."

"What about his father?" Kel asked, his voice tight and hard. "Doesn't he need his father? Or am I supposed to let Uncle Reed take care of that?"

"Reed has been a father figure of sorts, I guess." She looked away from the pain and anger in his green eyes, focusing on the toes of his cowboy boots instead. Reed's involvement in Michael's life was obviously a sore point with Kel. She was ashamed of the small part of her that wondered if Kel was jealous of the other man's involvement in *her* life. That wished he was?

"Reed's been very good to me," she said carefully. "And not in the way you keep implying," she added with a spurt of anger when she saw the look on his face. "Not that it's any of your business, but Reed has been a friend to me. Nothing more."

"Not by his choice, I'll bet."

Megan flushed but didn't deny it. The truth was, Reed was willing to be a great deal more than just a friend. The fact that their relationship hadn't moved past the friendship stage had been her choice. No matter how she tried, she had never been able to get past her memories of the man sitting in front of her.

"Reed has been very helpful, especially when I was sick. I don't know what Michael and I would have done without him."

If she'd been hoping to soften Kel's attitude toward the other man, she'd chosen the wrong way to go about it. He stood up with an abrupt movement that startled her. She pressed her back against the sofa, her eyes wary as she watched him walk to the window. She had no physical fear of him, but she was very conscious of the havoc he could wreak in her and Michael's life.

Kel curled the fingers of one hand around the curtain near his face as he stared out the window. Megan doubted he was admiring the newly green expanse of lawn.

"You shouldn't have had to rely on an outsider for help," he said without turning to look at her. "*I* am Michael's father. *I* should have been the one to take care of him. It was my responsibility."

Responsibility. Megan was glad his back was to her so he didn't see her wince at the word. It had to avoid being a responsibility that she'd left three years ago. And she'd chosen to keep the knowledge of his child from him because she couldn't bear the thought of either one of them being a responsibility in Kel's life.

But her illness had brought her face-to-face with how foolish she was being. It was ironic that a desire to avoid being Kel's responsibility had driven her to be irresponsible with her son's well-being. She only hoped that, in trying to rectify her mistake, she hadn't plunged the two of them into more trouble.

"It was being so sick that made me realize how wrong I'd been to keep Michael from you," she said. "I was afraid of what might happen to him if something happened to me."

"Hall said you nearly died."

Would you have cared if I had? The question was so strong in her mind that Megan lifted her hand to her mouth as if to physically prevent its escape.

"I was very sick," she admitted.

"How are you now? And don't tell me you're fine," he warned, turning to look at her with sharp eyes. "You look like a stiff wind would carry you off."

"You flatter me," she said with heavy sarcasm. When Kel only arched his brow in response, she sighed. "I'm fine." He opened his mouth to refute that statement but her lifted hand stopped him. "I'm fine for someone who's recovering from a bad bout of pneumonia," she clarified. "I'm still pretty shaky and I get tired easily. I don't normally pass out, though."

She thought Kel flushed a little at that, though she hadn't really intended the words as an accusation.

"What does the doctor have to say?"

"He says I'm going to be shaky and get tired easily." She shrugged and smiled a little. "It's just going to take time to get my strength back."

"What about your job?"

"Reed's hired someone to fill in for me for a few weeks."

"Is he paying you while you're not working?" There was an edge to the question that brought color to Megan's pale cheeks.

"He offered but I wouldn't let him."

"What about the rent on this place? Did he offer to waive that while you're getting back on your feet?"

"As a matter of fact, he did. And I didn't let him do that, either," she snapped. "Not that it's any of your business."

"That's where you're wrong. As the mother of my child, you're very much my business. I don't think it's unreasonable for me to want to know how you're managing financially. That has an effect on Michael's well-being, too."

"Michael is in no danger of going hungry or unclothed," she said sharply.

"I didn't say he was," Kel said, unperturbed by her annoyance.

He left the window and returned to the wing chair. Sitting down on the edge of it, he braced his elbows on his knees and bent his head to stare at his clasped hands. Megan stared at the top of his head. There were a few silver threads showing against the rich reddish brown. She curled her fingers into her palms, struggling against the urge to touch him.

She'd been so wrong to think that her feelings for this man were dead. They'd simply been buried away, covered over by the new life she'd worked to create. And all it had taken was to see him again to show her just how thin a facade she'd created.

"I want the two of you to move to the ranch."

Megan had been so absorbed in her thoughts that it took a second for her to realize what he'd said.

"What?" Not that she needed to hear it again. Kel must have known that because when he spoke, it wasn't to repeat his words.

"It's the perfect solution." He straightened up and looked at her.

"To what?" If she'd been sure her knees would support her, Megan would have stood up to pace the room. As it was, she stayed where she was, her wide eyes fixed on his face.

"You need rest. With Gracie at the ranch, you wouldn't have anything to do but rest. She'd like nothing better than to have a child to take care of."

"I can take care of my own child," she snapped, feeling as if control of her future—Michael's future—was slipping through her fingers.

"My child, too," he reminded her quietly. Megan wondered if it was her imagination that put a threat in those words. "I'm not talking about Gracie taking over and raising the boy."

"Good!"

"I'm just saying that she'd be there to give you a break now and then. I may not have spent a lot of time around two-year-olds but I doubt they're particularly restful."

That was putting it mildly. There were times when she felt as if she'd given birth to the Tasmanian devil. Just keeping up with Michael could be a full-time job. She'd never met Grace Cavenaugh, but from what Colleen had said, the woman had practically raised both her and Kel.

"I don't know," she muttered.

"I want a chance to get to know my son, Megan. You didn't think I'd just walk away once I found out about him, did you?"

"No. I knew you'd want to live up to your *responsibilities*." Despite her best efforts, she couldn't prevent the tiny edge that sharpened the word into something less than complimentary. She saw Kel frown and spoke before he could question her emphasis. "I assumed you'd want to visit occasionally."

"I have no intention of being an occasional father. I want to get to know Michael. I want him to get to know me. That isn't going to happen with a six-hour drive between us."

"I can't move to the ranch permanently," she said quickly, her mind reeling at the thought of being under the same roof with Kel Bryan even for a little while.

"We don't have to make any permanent decisions now," he said easily. "Why don't we start out with the two of you coming up for a couple of months? We'll work it out from there." He saw her hesitation and his voice hardened. "You owe me this, Megan."

Yes, she guessed she did owe him this much. He could certainly have demanded a great deal more and might do so if she refused to make this visit. It was just that the idea of spending the next two months in close proximity to him, of going to the ranch she'd grown to love—it was going to be like tearing open old wounds.

Kel waited for her decision. He didn't look particularly worried but then he probably knew he didn't have any reason to. He must know she had no real choice.

"All right," Megan said slowly. "We'll come stay at the ranch."

"Good." He stood up. "How much time do you need to get ready?"

"Two weeks?" She wanted to put it off as long as she could.

"Four days," he said flatly, recognizing her delaying tactic for what it was. "I'll be back on the weekend."

She nodded, resigned to her fate. She stood up and followed him out of the living room, but instead of going to the door, he hesitated in the hallway, glancing toward the back of the house. He couldn't have realized how much longing was revealed in his eyes. If he had, she was sure he wouldn't have let her see it.

"If you'd like to go take another look at Michael, he's the second door down," she said, as if the idea had occurred to her spontaneously. "He's a pretty heavy sleeper."

She slid her hands into the pockets of her skirt and stared unseeingly at the soft watercolor print that hung next to the kitchen door while she waited. She was very careful to keep her mind blank. There would be time enough to think later.

Kel wasn't gone long. "Thank you," he said quietly.

"You're welcome."

It struck her as ineffably sad that he should be thanking her for letting him look at his sleeping child, and she felt a wave of regret for the choices she'd made that had kept them apart. But saying she was sorry again wouldn't change anything.

She reached for the doorknob just as Kel did. His hand covered hers, and Megan felt her heartbeat catch as a wave of awareness swept up her arm and ran down her spine. It had been like this between them from the start, with even the smallest of touches creating sparks. She saw that same awareness in Kel's eyes.

For a moment, it seemed as if the past three years had disappeared. His head dipped toward hers. Did she lean toward him? Another breath, another heartbeat and their lips would touch.

Kel straightened abruptly, and his hand dropped away from hers as if burned. Megan pulled open the door and he stepped out onto the porch.

"I'll see you on Saturday," he said without looking at her.

"Saturday," she murmured, using the word as both confirmation and farewell. Megan pushed the door shut and leaned against it and closed her eyes.

She was going to be living with Kel again, seeing him every day. It was crazy, it could only lead to more heartache, but she couldn't prevent a little bubble of happiness from swelling up inside her.

Kel climbed into the sardine can of a rental car but he didn't immediately start the engine. Megan was back in his life. He wanted to believe that his only interest was in seeing his son but what he'd felt when he touched her a few moments ago had nothing to do with Michael. Crazy as it was, he still wanted her. The question was, what was he going to do about it?

Chapter 12

Kel refused Megan's offer to help with the driving, and neither of them had much inclination toward making light conversation. For the first couple of hours, Megan occupied herself with keeping Michael entertained. She'd been touched to see that Kel had purchased a car seat and installed it in his truck. She was even more touched by his seemingly endless patience with the toddler.

At his second meeting with his father, Michael had been a little less shy, though he still had his doubts about this large stranger. When the time came to climb into the truck, he'd shied away from allowing Kel to lift him up into the cab. With an apologetic look in Kel's direction, Megan had settled her son into his car seat.

Megan had never taken a long car trip with Michael and she wasn't sure what to expect. Six hours was a long time to keep a small boy cooped up in a car. She wondered if Kel had given that any thought when he decided to drive them from Cheyenne to the ranch. She wondered if he had any idea how whiny a two-year-old could get.

But if she expected him to be annoyed, she did him an injustice. As soon as Michael began to show signs of getting restless, Kel found a place to pull off the road so the child could run off some of his pent-up energy. It added quite a bit of time to the trip, but Kel showed no signs of impatience. In fact, he seemed content to just watch Michael, as if he was making up for the years he'd missed.

Near dark, Michael fell asleep, his head nodding in rhythm with the sound of the tires on the road. As evening closed in, narrowing her field of vision to what was visible in the headlights, Megan found herself falling into a state somewhere between sleep and wakefulness.

She'd dreamed of traveling this road so many times. Especially while she was pregnant, she'd fantasized about coming back to the ranch, carrying her baby, and of having Kel open his arms to both of them, not out of responsibility but out of love. After Michael was born, she'd had less time for daydreaming but the fantasy had remained in the back of her mind, even while she was busy telling herself that her love for Kel had faded for lack of nourishment.

"You're still in love with him, aren't you?" Reed had asked her when she told him that she and Michael would be spending a few weeks on the ranch.

"Don't be ridiculous." They were sitting in Reed's kitchen while he cooked dinner the evening after Kel's visit. Michael was playing on the kitchen floor, happily driving toy cars around the bottom of the skillet Reed had provided as a racetrack, garage or whatever.

Megan glanced up and met Reed's eyes for a moment and then occupied herself with carefully aligning her fork with the edge of her plate. "I'd be a fool to still be in love with him," she muttered.

"I could buy you a peaked hat and shoes that turn up at the toes," he offered. "Then you could dress the part."

"I'm not in love with him anymore." Megan enunciated each word very carefully. She caught his doubting look. "I'm not."

"When I was in third grade, I had to write on the blackboard one hundred times, I will not throw spitballs at Mary Kate Beldon," Reed said, apropos of nothing. "I guess the teacher figured writing it that many times would make it true." He glanced over his shoulder and grinned at her. "You want a blackboard, honey?"

"You are a repellent individual," she told him.

"I know." He sighed. "It's a cross I just have to bear."

Despite her inner turmoil, Megan had to smile, which was undoubtedly what he'd intended. She did love Reed, but as a friend rather than a lover. He'd made it clear that he wouldn't object to changing his status in her life but he'd never pushed the issue. Though he hadn't said as much, Megan had the feeling that Reed had suffered pain in the past. Certainly, his heart hadn't been broken when she'd chosen to remain his friend rather than become his lover.

She'd told herself several times that she was being foolish, that she should take what he offered and build a life for herself with one of the nicest men she was ever likely to meet. And maybe she would have, except she hadn't been able to shake the idea that she'd be doing Reed a disservice.

"I don't want to love him," she said, aware that she sounded about the same age as her son.

"And I don't want to be so witty and charming," Reed said. His drawl thickened dramatically as he added, "But as my grandpappy used to say, you just got to make do with what the good Lord provides, boy."

"I don't believe you had a grandpappy," she grumbled, reaching for her fork.

"Everybody has a grandpappy," Reed protested as he sat down across from her. "You think I was found under a sweet potato vine?"

"Did you really call him Grandpappy?"

"Well." He drew the word out. He looked at her and grinned. "Actually, he owned a highly successful law firm in Nashville and I never called him anything less dignified than Grandfather."

"And did he ever say any of those hokum truisms you always attribute to him?" she demanded.

"He would have if he'd thought of them," Reed temporized.

"So you've been lying to me all along." She shook her head sadly. "Another illusion shattered."

"Illusion is just another word for lying to yourself," he said, and Megan knew they'd returned to the subject of her feelings for Kel. "And you're too smart for that."

"Get off my case, Reed. I am not in love with Kel Bryan," she said stubbornly, hoping the words didn't sound as hollow to him as they did to her.

"I think you're going to need an extra box of chalk," he said sorrowfully.

Half asleep, Megan let the conversation drift through her head. If only writing something a hundred times could make it true, she thought lazily.

She roused as Kel turned the truck onto the ranch road, the tires biting into the gravel surface. It was too dark for her to see anything but she stared out the window anyway. Despite the circumstances, she couldn't entirely suppress a feeling of excitement. In the few short months she'd spent here, this place had become more of a home to her than anywhere else she'd lived. And despite the way it had ended, that summer had been the happiest time of her life.

When they came around a curve in the road and the ranch house was suddenly visible, Megan's heart jumped with pleasure.

"It looks just like I remember," she said and then bit her lip, wishing she hadn't spoken out loud. She felt Kel's glance but kept her eyes focused beyond the truck's nose.

"Things don't change much around here," he said after a moment.

He pulled the truck up in front of the house. As soon as he turned off the engine, the silence rushed in on them. Megan had almost forgotten the intensity of the quiet, a stillness so heavy it was almost a sound.

They sat there for a few seconds and she thought Kel looked as if he was about to say something. But if that was the case, he apparently changed his mind because he opened the door and got out. With a sigh for lost moments, Megan began unbuckling Michael from his car seat. She'd just eased him out of it when Kel opened the door on her side of the truck.

"Let me take him," he said quietly as she turned.

There was a slight, almost imperceptible hesitation on her part and then Megan leaned forward to allow him to take his son from her.

Kel was unprepared for the feeling that washed over him as he felt his son's weight in his arms. Tenderness and awe, regret and love all tangled together. He was so small, almost insubstantial.

"He won't break," Megan said, apparently reading his mind.

"He's so little." Kel shifted Michael to a more comfortable position in his arms as Megan stepped out of the truck.

"Actually, he's big for his age. The doctor says he'll probably be over six foot."

"The Bryan men have always been tall," Kel said, feeling a surge of possessive pride. This was his son, his flesh and blood. He smiled at the sleeping child. It didn't matter that he'd missed the first two years of the boy's life. It didn't matter that they were strangers to one another. Those things paled into insignificance beside the single fact that they were father and son, bonded on a blood-deep level in a way that could never be changed.

Seeing the look on Kel's face, Megan felt a mixture of joy—how could she not be glad that her son's father so obviously wanted him—and jealousy—Michael was *her* son and she wasn't accustomed to sharing. But joy or jealousy, anger or acceptance, there was no going back.

Grace Cavenaugh was nothing like Megan had pictured her. Rather than the short, round, jovial woman of her imagination, Mrs. Cavenaugh was tall and spare with a face right out of a Grant Wood painting. Megan didn't think it was her imagination or simply a natural reserve that put a cool edge to the older woman's greeting. But then, she supposed keeping Kel's child from him wasn't going to win her any friends on the Lazy B.

But Michael was another story. When she saw the sleeping child in Kel's arms, her somber face creased in a huge smile, all her reserve vanishing in an instant. Megan knew Kel had been right when he'd said that the housekeeper would be more than happy to keep an eye on Michael.

"He's the spitting image of you when you were his age," she said, peering at Michael. Kel grinned, clearly pleased by the comparison. "No doubt about who his daddy is."

Megan wondered if it was her imagination that the older woman sounded relieved. Had Gracie thought that she might have lied about Michael's paternity? She debated whether or not she should feel indignant and then decided it would require too much effort. Just standing here trying to look alert was taking every bit of energy she had.

It was ridiculous to be so tired when all she'd done all day was sit in the truck and watch Kel drive. But ridiculous or not, exhaustion was washing over her in waves, each more powerful than the last.

"I've soup heating, if you're hungry," Mrs. Cavenaugh said, looking from Kel to Megan.

"Thank you but I'm a little tired." Megan forced a smile and hoped she wouldn't mortally offend the woman by turning down her soup.

She thought she was managing to conceal the extent of her tiredness fairly well but when Kel glanced at her, he immediately saw the glazed look in her eyes. Her skin was so pale that it had an almost translucent look about it, except for the faint blue circles under her eyes. She was all but swaying on her feet.

"I'll show you to your room. I'll have some soup when I come down, Gracie," he said.

"If you'll just tell me which room it is, I'll take Michael up." Megan held out her arms but Kel was shaking his head.

"You look as if you'll be lucky to get yourself up the stairs, let alone Michael. I'll carry him." Even if she hadn't looked so tired, he was reluctant to give up his son just yet. He'd never in his life held anything that felt half so sweet. Except perhaps the child's mother. Kel pushed the thought aside, not sure he wanted to examine it too closely.

He shifted his hold on Michael, holding him so that his small body sprawled against his chest, which left him with one hand free to set against Megan's back, offering small support as she climbed the stairs. He thought it a good indication of her exhaustion that she didn't bother with even a token protest. When they reached the top of the stairs, she paused a moment, catching her breath.

"I feel so stupid, getting winded just climbing one flight of stairs," she muttered.

"You've been sick."

"No kidding."

Kel felt one corner of his mouth kick up at her rueful comment. One of the things he'd liked most about Megan was her sense of humor.

He felt Megan hesitate when he stopped outside her old room. Glancing at her, he saw her gaze drift across the hall to his door. He knew she had to be thinking about the nights they'd spent together, the passion they'd shared. As if against her will, her eyes met his and he saw the memories reflected there.

For a moment, there in the dimly lit hallway, it almost seemed as if it was three years ago. As if they were still lovers. He wanted to lift his hand and see if her hair was as soft as he remembered, to slide his fingers under the edge of her T-shirt and feel the soft skin of her belly quiver at his touch. Arousal stirred in him and from the sudden catch in Megan's breathing, he knew she felt the same thing.

If it hadn't been for the presence of the child in his arms, Kel might have given in to the urge to reach for Megan, to renew old memories. But Michael stirred against his shoulder, a vivid reminder that not all of those old memories were good memories. He turned and pushed open the door.

"I had Gracie set Colleen's old crib up in here. I thought you might want Michael in the same room, at least at first." He stepped back to let her enter and then followed her in. "Once he's settled in a bit, we can move him into the room next to this one."

"This looks fine." Megan lifted her hand to brush her hair from her face. The small movement seemed to take an enormous amount of energy. She sank onto the bed and let her eyes drift around the room. Aside from the crib in one corner, it looked the same as she remembered.

"I'll bring some of your things up from the truck," Kel said.

"All the essentials are in the red suitcase." She watched through bleary eyes as he walked toward her.

"I'll set him on the bed for now."

If she hadn't been so tired, Megan thought that the tenderness with which he set Michael on the bed beside her would have brought tears to her eyes.

"I'll be right back."

She thought she nodded but she wasn't sure. As soon as the door closed behind his tall figure, she sank back against the pillows. She'd just rest while he was gone. Just for a few minutes. She reached out and slid her arm around Michael, tugging him closer as her eyes drifted shut. Just for a few minutes...

Kel set the suitcase down inside the door and walked over to the bed. Megan lay on top of the covers, one arm curled protectively over Michael's small body, both of them sound asleep.

Mother and child. As perfect as a Norman Rockwell painting. Megan's fair hair was spread across the pillows, a vivid contrast to Michael's dark locks. His cheeks were flushed with sleep, his mouth slightly open. He looked as if, even in sleep, he knew he was safe and secure, just the way it should be, Kel thought.

He reached down to brush his fingertips over his son's rosy cheek, his smile gentle. He still found it hard to believe that he'd had a part in creating anything so perfect. His eyes shifted to Megan. She looked as pale and fragile as their son did healthy and sturdy.

He remembered Reed Hall's comment that she'd almost died. He'd been furious with her when he found out about Michael. He was still furious, but the thought of anything happening to her twisted his gut into a knot. And it wasn't just because she was the mother of his child. It was something deeper and more visceral.

Kel frowned and straightened away from the bed. He reached for the quilt folded across the foot of the bed and pulled it up over the sleeping pair. Snapping off the bedside lamp, he left the room without looking back.

When Megan thought about it, which was fairly often, she was amazed at how easily both she and Michael made the transition to living on the ranch.

She pushed the toes of one foot against the porch floor, setting the glider in motion. If she closed her eyes, it was almost possible to believe that it was three summers ago and that everything was just as it had been. But it wasn't.

Opening her eyes, Megan watched Michael stirring a stick in the soil at the edge of the rose bed. Carey Wills and Dick Brownwell had shown up the day after they arrived and strung chicken wire around the exterior of the split rail fence that already enclosed the yard, making it impossible for an adventurous toddler to slip between the rails and get into the ranch yard itself. They'd tipped their hats to her but hadn't made any effort at conversation. Megan couldn't help but wonder if it was just a cowboy's natural reticence or if they thought she'd committed an unpardonable crime by keeping Kel's child from him.

Not that she could blame them if they did, Megan admitted with a sigh. When she saw how patient Kel was with Michael and the obvious love that softened his face whenever he saw his son, she wondered that she could have made the choices she had. Of course, the truth was, she hadn't so much made choices as she had taken the path of least resistance. When she'd left, she'd told herself that she'd get in touch with Kel. Only it had been easier not to open that particular door so she'd left it closed.

She sighed again. Maybe if Colleen were here… But Colleen probably blamed her more than anyone else. She and Kel were very close and anyone who hurt her older brother wasn't likely to be a favorite of Colleen's, so maybe it was just as well that she was spending the summer at a friend's thoroughbred ranch in Kentucky.

"Mommy." Michael's demand for attention dragged Megan out of her thoughts. Smiling, she stood and walked down the porch steps to crouch next to him and exclaim over the hole he'd dug. Inspired by her admiration, Michael demonstrated his hole digging abilities again. Megan silently promised the roses a prompt restoration of their quarters when her son took a nap and tried not to think just how filthy he was getting.

"Digging for worms?"

Kel's voice came from the other side of the fence, and Megan tilted her head to look up at him. He was sitting astride Dude—another thing that hadn't changed—looking at the two of them, his mustache quirked in an indulgent smile.

"Don't suggest it," she said. "He'd probably eat any he found."

She stood up, dusting her hands against the seat of her jeans. She looked better than she had two weeks ago, Kel thought, looking at her critically. There was some color in her cheeks and she'd put on a little weight. She was still too thin, and though she never said anything, he knew she still tired easily. But she was definitely on the mend and looking more desirable all the time, he admitted reluctantly.

Her eyes met his and awareness flashed between them, the way it always had, the way he was starting to think it always would. From the start, she'd affected him like no woman ever had, and three years' absence hadn't changed that. Not even his anger over losing the first two years of his son's life could change that. He saw the color rise in her cheeks and knew he wasn't the only one to feel the spark of attraction between them.

"Up." Michael's voice broke the tension between his parents. "Horse. Up." Just in case he hadn't managed to get the message across, he held his arms up toward Kel.

"You're too little, honey," Megan said, bending to pick him up.

"Daddy, up." He leaned out of her arms, stretching toward Kel.

The first few days after they arrived at the Lazy B, Michael had kept a wary eye on Kel but he'd gradually figured out that, despite his size and the deepness of his voice, Kel was as much his slave as the other adults in his small world. Kel didn't know if the boy had any grasp at all of the fact that Daddy meant something more significant than Gracie, but every time he heard the word, something melted inside him.

"Let me take him up in front of me," Kel said.

"He's only two," Megan protested.

"I was younger than he is the first time my father took me up with him," Kel said.

She hesitated, her eyes flickering uneasily over Dude's large frame. Kel waited. He was Michael's father but he deferred to her authority when it came to the boy.

"I won't let anything happen to him," he said quietly.

"I know." But she still hesitated.

Michael bounced in her arms, impatient with the delay. As far as he was concerned, there was no decision to make. He wanted to ride the horse and it didn't occur to him that anyone might object.

"Ride," he demanded.

"All right." With an uncertain laugh, Megan lifted him. Kel leaned from the saddle, his fingers brushing against hers as he took the boy from her.

The minute she felt Michael's weight leave her hands, Megan wanted to snatch him back. He was too little. What if the horse bucked him off? What if he bolted? The fact that Dude stood steady as a rock, placidly switching flies with his tail, did nothing to reassure her.

She bit her lip, watching as Kel settled Michael in front of him. He looked so tiny atop the black horse, his father's big body behind him. He stared at the back of Dude's head, his eyes big as saucers. Kel had one hand against his chest and Michael's fingers clutched at his arm while he debated the results of his demand.

He cast his mother an uncertain look, hovering on the verge of changing his mind, and Megan did her best to give him an encouraging smile.

"What do you think?" Kel asked, his deep voice gentle as he leaned over the boy. The sound of Kel's voice seemed to reassure him. His response was nonverbal but quite clear. His tiny legs kicked impatiently. He knew horses moved, and now that he was on one, he wanted to do something besides sit. Grinning, Kel nudged Dude with his heel and the big horse moved off at a slow amble.

Megan stood next to the fence, her hands clasped against her chest, tears blurring her vision as she looked at the two people she loved most in all the world. Reed had been right. She could write a denial on a blackboard a thousand times but nothing would change the truth. She still loved Kel Bryan.

That evening, after putting Michael down for the night, Megan wandered downstairs. She was too restless to read or watch television. Gracie generally retired to her own quarters as soon as the kitchen was tidied after supper. Not that Megan was much inclined to seek her out for conversation. In the past two weeks, they'd rubbed along pretty well together but they were far from being best buddies. There was a light on under the door to Kel's study but she was even less inclined to seek him out.

Without bothering to turn the light on, she drifted out onto the front porch and settled into her favorite spot on the glider. A three-quarter moon rode high overhead, casting light and shadow over the landscape. Megan rested her chin on her updrawn knees and let her mind wander.

She had no idea how long she'd been sitting there when she felt the glider shudder as Kel sat down next to her. As usual, he hadn't made a sound but she wasn't startled by his arrival. She felt almost as if she'd been waiting for him.

"You're very good with Michael," she said, without turning her head.

"Thank you. It's not hard. He's a great little kid. Not afraid of anything."

"He'd probably put his head in a tiger's mouth if he thought there might be something interesting to see," she agreed. She turned her head to smile at him.

"Probably." Kel's smile held both amusement and pride. "Another year or two and I'll have to see about getting him a pony of his own."

Megan opened her mouth to protest that he'd be too young and then closed it without saying anything. There'd be time enough to argue when the time came and she didn't want anything to spoil the peaceful moment. But Kel must have read her mind.

"I won't let anything happen to him, Megan," he said quietly. "He's my son, too."

"I know." She sighed, feeling her peaceful mood slipping away. "It's just that it's been just the two of us since he was born."

"What about Reed Hall?"

"I've already told you that Reed is just a friend."

"So you said." He didn't trouble to hide his doubt.

"So I meant," she said firmly. "I've been the only one to have any say in Michael's life and it's not easy giving up even a part of that control to someone else."

She half expected him to make some angry reference to the fact that she'd kept him apart from Michael, but he surprised her by nodding slowly.

"I understand that. I know it's going to take time. For all of us. But I *am* Michael's father and I have every intention of living up to that responsibility."

"I know." With a single word, he'd finished spoiling her mood. Responsibility. Why was it that, with Kel, she was annoyed by what she'd respect in anyone else? *Because you want to be so much more than a responsibility to him,* a small voice inside answered.

With a sigh, she stood up. "I think I'll go in now."

Kel rose to his feet as she walked by and she caught her breath as her arm brushed against his. She glanced into his face but the light was too poor for her to be able to see his expression.

"G-good night," she said, her voice a little too breathless. She squeaked, startled by the feel of his hand closing around her upper arm.

"Maybe we should just get it out of the way," he said, his voice husky. He took hold of her other arm and turned her toward him.

"Get what out of the way?" Megan had to clear her throat before she could get the question out. Her heart was beating much too quickly and she couldn't prevent her eyes from drifting to his mouth.

"This," he said against her lips.

It was just the way he remembered it. One touch and heat flared to life between them. His tongue traced the fullness of her bottom lip, and with a sigh she opened to him, inviting him inside. It was an invitation he didn't hesitate to accept.

Megan's hands came up, her fingers clutching his shirt for support as her knees weakened. This was what she'd been waiting for ever since he came back into her life. This was what she'd missed for the past three years, this feeling of completion that she seemed to find only in his arms. Heat pooled in the pit of her stomach, a warm urgency that had her crowding closer to him as his tongue slid into her mouth, claiming her for his own.

Kel felt her total surrender and groaned softly. If he chose to lay her out on the porch floor and take her right then and there, he knew she wouldn't offer a whisper of protest. The image did nothing to cool the temperature of his blood.

One hand flattened against her back, crushing her against his hard body. He'd never known anything like the hunger she created in him. Kissing her was like tasting a piece of heaven, like coming home, like finding a part of himself he hadn't known was missing.

With a groan of protest, he dragged his mouth free and leaned his forehead against hers. They stood that way for a few seconds, Megan's body draped against his, the only sound the harsh rasp of their breathing.

"If we don't stop this now, you're going to end up with your skirt shoved up and your legs around my waist," he whispered raggedly.

Megan's gasp wasn't entirely one of shock at his blunt words. The image he'd painted added to the ache in the pit of her stomach, and for an instant she wanted nothing more than to find herself in exactly the position he'd described.

You're falling right back into the same trap, she thought. And it would end the same way it had last time, with her heart getting battered again. Only this time, she had to consider Michael. For better or worse, she and Kel were forever linked by their son. This time, she wouldn't be able to run away.

"I think I should go in now," she whispered, pushing away from him.

"That's probably safest," he said, letting her go.

She hesitated a moment longer. Safe wasn't exactly what she wanted right now. But what she wanted and what she could have were two very different things.

With a last look at Kel, Megan turned and went into the house, hurrying up the stairs as if running away. Not that it did her any good, she thought as she slipped into the room she shared with Michael. Because she couldn't run fast enough to escape herself.

Chapter 13

Megan approached the kitchen a little warily. After their encounter the night before, she wasn't particularly anxious to see Kel, at least not before she'd had her first cup of coffee. She'd have delayed longer but Michael was awake and wanted his breakfast. With him perched on her hip, she eased her way through the kitchen door. Gracie was standing at the sink, her back to the door and there was no sign of—

"He's long gone so you can stop sneaking around," Gracie said without turning.

"I wasn't sneaking," Megan said. She came into the kitchen and settled Michael into his high chair. "And I don't have any reason to avoid Kel."

She did her best to look unperturbed as Gracie turned from the sink, drying her hands on the towel she wore looped through her apron strings.

"Suppose you got that whisker burn running into a wall," Gracie said, her faded blue eyes shrewd.

Megan immediately put her hand to her face. She'd thought the slightly pink tone of her cheek was unnoticeable. But she should have known better than to think she could get anything by Grace Cavenaugh.

"Did Kel or Colleen ever manage to get anything by you?" she asked ruefully.

"Not much. There's coffee in the maker. You look like you could use a cup. I've got the little one's cereal ready. Sit yourself down."

Megan did as she was told. While she was getting her coffee, Gracie set Michael's cereal and half a banana on the tray. Megan sat down and took a sip of her coffee, shuddering as the thick brew hit her palate.

"Coffee too strong for you?" Gracie asked.

"Got a horseshoe I can try floating in it?" Megan's smile was rueful. "The first time I met Kel, he said that was the test of good coffee."

"Ought to be strong enough to put hair on your chest," Gracie agreed, pouring herself a cup and sitting down across from Megan.

"Strong as this stuff is, I ought to look like Tom Selleck pretty soon."

It was the first time she'd heard Gracie laugh. The sound was much lighter and more girlish than she would have expected. Megan smiled, feeling her mood lighten a bit. Maybe she and Gracie would end up friends after all. A moment later, she wasn't so sure.

"You still planning on leaving in a couple of weeks?"

"I . . . assume so." Megan took another sip of coffee and fixed her attention on Michael, as if she wanted to learn the secret of mashing bananas with a spoon.

"Taking the little one with you?"

"Of course!" She shot Gracie a quick look, surprised she'd even ask such a question.

Gracie nodded. She picked up her coffee cup, lifted it partway to her mouth and then set it down again, staring at it a moment as if not sure how it came to be in front of her. From what Megan had seen, such indecision was not normal for the other woman.

"Kel ever tell you about his mother?" The question appeared to be a non sequitur, but Megan was sure Gracie had a reason for asking it.

"No. Colleen told me she left when Colleen was just a baby. Other than that, I don't recall any mention of her."

"There wouldn't have been." Gracie stared into her coffee cup and Megan had the feeling that she was holding some sort of debate with herself. She appeared to come to some decision because she sighed and began to speak.

"Truth is, the only good thing that woman ever did in her life was have those two children. I came here right after they were married because Susan was too delicate to take care of this house. Delicate." She snorted. "Woman was about as delicate as a barracuda and had a temper to match. Beautiful, though. Red hair, green eyes—if a body wanted to paint a temptress, Susan Bryan would have made a good model."

Megan's coffee sat untouched in front of her as she listened, fascinated by this sudden spate of information.

"My husband and I hadn't been married long and he came to work for Kel's daddy same time I came to work in the house. It was obvious pretty quick that the boss's new wife wasn't particularly suited to living here. She wanted clothes and parties, to see and be seen. Nothin' wrong with that, I guess," she added, obviously attempting to be fair. "But a working ranch ain't the place to find that sort of thing."

She stopped and Megan waited, hardly breathing, afraid that she wasn't going to hear the rest of the story. But after a moment, Gracie went on.

"Kel loved her, of course. She was beautiful and glamorous and fond enough of the boy, 'specially since he worshiped her. He was about five the first time she left. She was gone a year or so, came back for six months, long enough to sink her claws into the two of them and then took off again. That's pretty much the way it went for the next six or seven years. She was gone more often than not, but just about the time you'd start to think she was gone for good, she'd turn up like a bad penny."

"It must have been very difficult for Kel and for his father," Megan said, trying to imagine what it would be like to have a parent like that. She wondered if the total abandonment she'd experienced might not have been kinder in the long run. At least she hadn't had her hopes raised again and again, only to see them dashed.

"It was pure hell," Gracie said bluntly. "Colleen was born a few months after one of Susan's visits. She brought the baby home, stayed a few weeks and then took off again. She didn't visit as much after that, every few years, maybe. Colleen hardly knew her and didn't seem to mind it much. I think it was harder for Kel.

"Last time Susan came home, Colleen was eight or so. And this time, Patrick, Kel's daddy, he told her not to come back again, that he was filing for divorce and that she could stay the hell out of all their lives." Gracie shifted the coffee cup back and forth between her hands, watching the motion.

"I guess she never thought he'd get to that point, and she was madder than a wet hen about having her little game ended. Ran into Colleen on the way out of the house and told the girl that Patrick might not be her real father. Did it out of pure spite, trying to get back at Patrick."

Megan gasped, finding it hard to believe that any woman could be so cruel to her own child. She reached out to touch Michael's shoulder, more to reassure herself than him. He looked at her and gave her a toothy, mashed-banana-and-cereal smile that only a mother could have loved.

"Colleen was upset but Patrick told her she was not to think about it. She was his daughter and that was that. She was young enough, I guess, to accept his word for it. But Kel never forgave his mother. She showed up for Patrick's funeral a few years later and Kel threw her out, told her if he ever saw her again, he wouldn't be held responsible for his actions."

"I can't blame him," Megan said.

"No. But it's hard on a boy to hate his mother like that, even if she deserves it. And then he upped and married a girl who was Susan's spitting image. Oh, not her malice. There aren't many women who could match Susan there. But Roxanne was no more suited to living on a ranch than his mother had been. Pretty as a picture and useless as tits on a boar hog,'' Gracie summed up bluntly.

"Was he . . . Did he love her very much?"

"No." The flat answer brought Megan's eyes to the older woman's face. "I think he was just as glad to see her go as she was to be going. But she didn't do anything to make him trust his own feelings when it comes to women."

Megan kept her eyes on Michael, who was happily smearing cereal from one end of the metal tray to another. When the silence continued to stretch, she sighed and looked at the older woman.

"Why did you tell me this?" She thought she could guess the answer.

"Because I thought it might help you to know the reasons if Kel isn't very good at saying what he's feeling. I don't normally gossip, but that boy means as much to me as if he were my own son, and I'd hate to see him lose out on a chance for happiness just because he doesn't have the sense to ask for what he wants."

She didn't seem to expect an answer, which was just as well because Megan wasn't sure she could have come up with one. She stayed where she was when Gracie got up and lifted Michael out of his high chair, muttering about him wearing more food than he ate. Michael grinned at her, well aware that Gracie was his adoring slave.

Megan stared into the murky depths of her coffee cup, aware of a dull pain somewhere behind her breastbone. Funny, how much it hurt to have Gracie imply that Kel loved her and just couldn't say the words. If only that were true.

With a sigh, she stood up and turned to take a freshly washed Michael from Gracie's strong hands. She gave the older woman what she hoped was a reassuring smile. It was too bad that Gracie's romantic fantasies were destined for disappointment. And it was too bad that her own heart was destined to be broken again.

It had been a long time since Kel had felt so much personal turmoil. Having Michael in his life had filled an emptiness he hadn't even known was there. He loved the boy more than he'd have believed possible. From his rich, little-boy laugh to his talent for getting into mischief, Kel was convinced there was no more perfect child in the state of Wyoming.

His feelings for Michael's mother were considerably less straightforward. There was a lingering anger over the way she'd kept Michael from him, but the more time he spent around her, the more he found himself thinking of how she brightened his life, remembering how empty the house had seemed after she'd left three years ago. And since the kiss they'd shared two weeks ago, he'd been vividly reminded of just how empty his bed had seemed without her.

The steady rhythm of the currybrush across Dude's flank faltered as Kel stared across the animal's back at the wall of the barn. It wasn't just the house or even his bed that had felt empty. It was his life. If Michael filled up an empty place he'd never known he had, then Megan filled one that had been there as long as he could remember.

She made him want to believe in things he'd long ago decided weren't in the cards for him. Things like love. And marriage. Things like happily ever after. Things that were likely to leave him with an aching hole in his gut when she left. And what did that say about what he felt for her?

Kel shied away from the question, more than a little afraid he wouldn't like the answer. He reached up to scratch Dude behind the ear. "You don't know how easy you've got it, buddy." Dude snorted, as if to say that Kel wasn't telling him anything he didn't already know.

Kel put away the currycomb and let himself out of the stall. It was almost dinnertime so he went up to the house to shower before the meal. He'd just pushed open his bedroom door when he heard the sound of Michael's laughter coming from the room across the hall. An instant later, he heard Megan laugh, a happy, young sound he'd heard all too little of lately. As if that laughter was a magnet, he turned toward it, his mouth curving.

Megan's door was partially open. She didn't notice when he pushed it a few more inches and stepped into the doorway. She and Michael were wrestling on the bed. As near as he could tell from the tangle of arms and legs, Megan was trying to put a pair of pants on her son and he was trying equally hard to avoid that fate. From the giggles and laughter, it was obvious that neither of them was taking the battle seriously.

Kel leaned his shoulder against the doorjamb and enjoyed the scene before him. This was how it should be, he thought. The only thing he would have changed was to add himself to the picture. But Megan had been so skittish around him since that kiss that he knew his presence would only spoil the moment. He started to step back and leave them to their play, but Michael's bright eyes had found him.

"Daddy!" His shrill cry held nothing but welcome, and Kel felt the familiar melting sensation in his chest. Megan threw him a startled look and quickly sat up, releasing Michael, who promptly scrambled off the bed and ran to his father.

"Hi, sport." Kel caught him under the arms and swung the boy up over his head, grinning at the delighted shriek this evoked. "Looks like you just about had your mother buffaloed."

Michael didn't know what buffaloed meant but he proceeded to explain in detail his strategy for winning the Battle of the Pants. At least that's what Kel assumed he was discussing. Michael's thoughts were inclined to run ahead of his available vocabulary, which made conversations with him largely a game of fill in the blanks.

Watching the two of them together, Megan had to blink back tears. Kel listened carefully to what Michael was saying. With their heads together, the resemblance between the two of them was striking. No one could ever mistake them for anything other than father and son.

"How about you get dressed for supper, now?" Kel said, after expressing appropriate admiration for his son's efforts to avoid his fate. Michael looked dubious about this idea as Kel carried him over to where Megan still sat on the bed.

"You think between the two of us, we can get a pair of pants on this one?" he asked.

"I don't know. He may be tougher than both of us."

Kel dangled Michael in midair while Megan threaded the pants on his legs. Since Michael decided that kicking his legs made the game much more interesting, this wasn't as easy as it might have been. But civilization triumphed and the small pants were finally in place.

"Stubborn little cuss, isn't he," Kel said. He bent to rub his nose against Michael's neck, eliciting peals of laughter.

"Takes after his father," Megan said, smiling as she stood up.

"Me?" He widened his eyes in shock. "Not a stubborn bone in my body," he protested.

"Of course not." Megan's look was patently disbelieving. "Give me the imp and I'll see if I can get a comb near that head of his."

"I guess I'd better go get cleaned up. If I show up like this, Gracie will cut off my end of the table."

He started to hand Michael over to her, but during the transfer, Michael shifted abruptly, flinging his arms around his mother's neck, and the back of Kel's hand ended up pressed firmly against Megan's breast. Megan froze, her eyes flying to his face.

In an instant, all the tension was back between them. All the unspoken wants, the unfulfilled needs suddenly crackled in the air like lightning. Megan felt her nipple tighten and knew that Kel couldn't possibly miss the small betrayal. She saw the hunger in his eyes and knew that, if it hadn't been for Michael's presence, they'd already be on the bed.

Kel's hand moved, sliding from between her body and Michael's with agonizing slowness. They stared at each other, and Megan wondered if he could hear the rapid beat of her pulse, if he could sense that her body was more than ready to receive his. For an instant, she wished her son was anywhere but where he was. If only she and Kel were alone, this aching hunger could be assuaged.

"Down." Michael's demand was punctuated by an impatient wiggle and the moment was broken.

"I'll see you at dinner," Kel said, his voice a little rougher than usual.

"Yes." Megan bent to set Michael on the floor and didn't lift her head until she heard the door shut behind Kel. She took a deep, shuddering breath and pressed her hands to her flushed cheeks, carefully avoiding her reflection in the mirror over the dresser. She didn't want to see the stars in her eyes or the fear that lay behind them.

Megan poured milk into a small saucepan and set it on the stove to heat. Around her, the house was quiet, asleep, just as she should have been, she reminded herself. It was one o'clock in the morning and she should have been sound asleep instead of tiptoeing around the kitchen making cocoa. But three hours of tossing and turning had gained her nothing but a tangled bed and the threat of a headache.

She got out a mug and spooned cocoa and sugar into it, stirring the two together. The weather report had made no mention of a storm in the offing, but the way her skin tingled suggested otherwise. Of course, her storm had a name.

Kel Bryan.

Megan rubbed her hands over her upper arms, her eyes focusing on nothing in particular. She could still feel the pressure of his hand against her breast as if the imprint of it had been burned into her skin. All through dinner, she'd been acutely aware of him, of his every move.

Her stomach tight with tension, she'd barely touched her meal and had to fend off Gracie's concerned inquiries and comments about how she needed more meat on her bones. She'd seen Kel's gaze wander over her as if to check the accuracy of Gracie's words, and when he'd lifted his gaze to her face, the look in his eyes had expressed nothing but approval. The bones that so worried Gracie had nearly melted.

"Up kind of late, aren't you?"

At the sound of Kel's quiet voice, Megan shivered and closed her eyes. She wasn't surprised that he was here, she realized. It was as if she'd been expecting him all along.

"I couldn't sleep," she said, turning to face him. Not a good idea, she decided immediately.

She hadn't bothered to turn on any lights except one over the counter. In the shadowy light, he looked very large and very male. He must have gotten out of bed. He'd tugged on a pair of jeans, which he'd zipped but hadn't bothered to snap. His chest was bare, and Megan felt her mouth go dry as her eyes clung to the broad-muscled width of his shoulders.

"I couldn't sleep, either," he said. He came farther into the kitchen, pausing by the stove to turn the burner off under her milk.

"I was going to make cocoa," she said, hardly aware of her words. "I thought it might help me sleep."

"I know a better cure for insomnia." His voice was low and deep and Megan felt a throbbing begin in the pit of her stomach.

"You do?"

"A sure cure." He stopped in front of her, so close that she could feel the heat radiating off his body. She could see the glitter of his eyes. She swallowed hard.

"Maybe you should patent it," she whispered.

"Maybe I should."

Without ceremony, he brought his hands up and closed his fingers over her breasts. Megan arched her back, thrusting herself more firmly into his hold. This was what she'd been wanting ever since she'd come back to the ranch. The single kiss they'd shared had only added fuel to the fire.

"I heard you get up and followed you downstairs," Kel said. His thumbs brushed over her nipples, fiery hot through the thin cotton of her nightgown. She shuddered, her knees trembling. "I can't sleep for thinking about you, Megan. I lay in bed and think about having you naked beneath me, about being inside you, feeling your sweet, slick muscles holding me."

"Please." She hardly knew what she was asking for. For him to stop torturing her with words and kiss her? For him to rip her nightgown out of the way so she could feel his hands on her skin? Or for him to skip everything else and simply take her where they stood?

He reached out and caught her hand, bringing it to the front of his jeans so that she could feel the swollen length of him straining against the denim.

"That's what thinking about you does to me," he whispered, rocking his hips against her hand.

Whimpering, Megan fumbled for the tab of his zipper, wanting to feel the silken heat of him in her hand. She didn't care where they were or who might walk in on them. All she cared about was putting an end to the sweet torture.

But Kel was not quite so lost to their surroundings. He had no intention of having their lovemaking interrupted by Gracie coming out to see what the commotion was in her kitchen. He caught Megan's hand and dragged it away from him. If she kept touching him like that, he wasn't going to give a damn if the whole ranch walked in on them.

"Shh." He smothered her frustrated whimper with his mouth and bent to scoop her up into his arms.

By the time he'd carried her upstairs and into the privacy of his room, they were both nearly frantic with need. He wanted to take it slow, make it last forever, but the hunger was too powerful. Kel barely managed to get her nightgown and his jeans off and then they were tumbling on the bed, Megan's legs opening to him.

With a groan, Kel sheathed himself in her. Her hips arched, her heels digging into the sheets as she struggled to take him as deeply as possible. He thrust once, twice and the explosion hit with the force of a freight train, rocking them both, startling a muffled scream from her as her body convulsed beneath him, around him.

Resting his forehead on the pillow, Kel sucked in a ragged breath, his big body trembling with the force of his climax. It wasn't enough, he thought, almost despairingly. He was still hard and aching, still wanting her. He rocked his hips against her, hearing her whimper in response, feeling her fingers dig into his back as she arched against him. This time, he was going to make it last.

There was no storm outside like there had been the first time they'd come together, but the storm inside was as fierce as anything Mother Nature could have conjured. It went on and on, with Kel controlling the moment, controlling her body as well as his own. He took her to the edge again and again, only to pull her back, petting and soothing her until she stopped trembling only to start the climb again.

In the end, Megan all but fought him for control of their lovemaking, and Kel let her take it, let her push him onto his back and lower herself onto his aching arousal. All the foreplay made their lovemaking hard and fast. Kel's hands were bruising on her hips. Megan's fingernails left marks on his shoulders. And the final shuddering moment left them both drained and exhausted.

Megan collapsed onto his chest, her breath shuddering in and out of her. Neither of them spoke. Words would have been an intrusion. Kel ran his hand up and down her narrow back, savoring the feel of her lying along his body. Her breathing gradually slowed, and he felt her relax against him and knew she slept.

He remembered his words about having a cure for insomnia, and his mouth curved in a smile. *Looks like I was right*, he thought, closing his eyes and letting himself drift to sleep.

Chapter 14

They woke in the quiet hour just before dawn, and without exchanging a word made love again. This time it was slow and sweet, as powerful in its own way as their almost violent coming together the night before.

Afterward, holding Megan, Kel felt a peace like he'd never known before. For the first time in a long time, he was starting to believe that everything was going to work out. Maybe happily ever after wasn't quite the impossibility he'd thought.

She loved him. He was almost sure of it. She'd given herself too completely for it to be anything else. A woman who kept her virginity until she was twenty-five didn't give herself as utterly as Megan had just done unless her heart was involved.

"Marry me." He hadn't planned on saying the words. But once they were out, he didn't think he'd ever said anything that felt more right. "Marry me, Megan."

She stiffened against him but didn't say anything. Kel was so caught up in his own feeling of rightness that he hardly noticed her silence.

"We should have done it weeks ago. Hell, we should have done it three years ago, and would have, if I'd known you were pregnant." Somewhere along the way, he'd let go of his anger over that. It didn't matter anymore. What was past was past. What mattered was the future.

"We should be a family, you and me and Michael."

"We are a family," she said at last. She eased away from him and sat up. "You don't have to marry me for that."

"Yes, I do." He looked at her, but all he could see was her back and the pale fall of her hair. Couldn't she feel how right this was? "Michael's my son, Megan. You're his mother. I want to take care of both of you."

"You can take care of Michael without marrying me," she said.

"But I *want* to marry you. Hell, Megan, most women would think I *ought* to marry them," he said with a half laugh.

"I'm not most women." She stood up and went to where her nightgown lay half beneath his jeans on the floor.

Kel watched her untangle the two garments, feeling uneasiness push aside his earlier contentment. This wasn't exactly the reaction he'd anticipated. He hadn't necessarily expected her to shout an immediate yes. Women always seemed to want to discuss things before coming up with an answer, and she'd want to be sure it was the right thing for Michael. But he certainly hadn't expected this oddly flat reaction.

He stood up as she tugged her nightgown on over her head. Unconcerned with his nudity, he went to her, catching her hands in his and tugging her around to face him. She kept her eyes firmly on his chest.

"Are you going to leave without giving me an answer?" he asked lightly, hoping it was his imagination that something was wrong here.

"I can't."

"Can't marry me or can't give me an answer?"

Can't marry you, Megan thought but she couldn't get the words out. Couldn't bring herself to turn away from that dream.

"I can't give you an answer," she whispered. "I...I need some time, Kel." She lifted her eyes to his face and forced a half smile. "It's a big decision and I have to consider what's best for Michael, for all of us."

"This *is* what's best for all of us," he said quickly.

"I need time," she repeated. *Time to pull together the strength to say no.*

"All right." Reluctantly, he let his hands drop from hers. "Take the time you need."

"Thank you." She glanced over his shoulder. The sun had crept over the horizon, flooding the room with light and she hoped he'd attribute the brightness of her eyes to its brilliance. "I have to go. Michael will be up soon."

She turned to go but Kel's hands caught her up against him. Her head fell back, her mouth softening under the impact of his kiss. He released her as suddenly as he'd grabbed her.

"Just thought I'd give you something to remember," he said, smiling at her.

She lifted trembling fingers to her mouth. "I won't forget."

And then she was gone, pulling the door quietly closed behind her. Kel frowned after her. Something didn't feel quite right. He wanted to go after her and drag her into his arms and kiss her until she admitted she loved him and agreed to marry him. He shook his head, forcing himself to turn away from the door. He'd said he'd give her time and he would. He just hoped she didn't make him wait too long.

Kel swung out of the saddle and looped Dude's reins around the top rail of the corral fence. It was the middle of the afternoon, and he should have been repairing fence on the south pasture. He *had* been doing just that since leaving the house this morning.

But all morning he'd had the feeling that something was wrong. In fact, he hadn't been able to get the idea out of his head since Megan walked out of his room just after dawn. Telling himself it was only natural that she should be on his mind hadn't helped. And he'd finally given in to the compulsion to leave his men to repair the fence and ride to the ranch.

The first thing he looked for was her car, which he'd towed behind the truck all the way from Cheyenne. He sagged with relief when he saw it, only then realizing just how much he'd feared that it would be gone and Megan and Michael with it.

From the corral, he could see that Gracie was in the garden, and Michael's small figure darted around her like a minnow circling a rock. He smiled as he headed

up to the house. As long as Gracie was around, they
wouldn't have to worry about Michael's lack of
grandparents.

Once they were married, everything would settle
into place. Megan had to see how right it would be.
How right *they* would be. He tried to ignore the uneasiness in the pit of his stomach.

Kel pushed open the front door and stepped into the
cool dimness of the house. A quick glance in the living room and kitchen told him that Megan wasn't
downstairs. Maybe she was taking a nap. She still tired
more easily than she liked to admit.

He walked quietly up the stairs and down the hall to
the room she shared with Michael. Once they were
married, she would move across the hall into his room
and this room could become Michael's alone. They'd
be close by in case he needed them but they'd still have
their privacy. He had every intention of needing a
great deal of privacy.

The door was open a crack and Kel pushed it open,
not wanting to wake Megan if she was asleep. He
needn't have worried. She wasn't asleep. She was bent
over the bed, carefully folding garments and placing
them into her open suitcase.

Kel was momentarily frozen. Vaguely, he was aware
of a sharp ache in his chest, a feeling of impending loss
so great it was like a crater opening up inside him. She
was leaving.

Again.

"What the hell are you doing?" At his question,
Megan jumped and spun around, one hand pressed
against her chest as if to still the sudden pounding of
her heart, and stared at him in utter dismay.

When she seemed at a loss for words, Kel walked into the room and pushed the door shut behind him. Giving himself a few seconds to think, he pulled off his hat and turned to hang it carefully on one corner of Michael's crib. Staring at the cartoon figures that decorated the sheet, he ran his fingers through his flattened hair. There was a crack opening up in his chest, a familiar emptiness in the pit of his stomach.

"Where are you going?" he asked quietly, careful to keep the desolation from his voice. He'd almost believed, almost thought it possible...

"Cheyenne," she said in a voice so low he had to strain to hear it. He turned to look at her. She looked nearly as pale as she had when he first saw her a few weeks ago, and her eyes were smoky blue with distress.

"Back to Hall?"

"No." She combed her fingers through her hair and then let her hand drop limply to her side. She looked as miserable as he felt. Too bad it wasn't for the same reason. "Only in the sense that he happens to be my landlord and my employer. I've told you before that there's nothing more than friendship between Reed and me."

Kel nodded. He almost wished he didn't believe her. It might have made it easier if he'd thought she was going to another man.

"Why are you going?" He was a fool to ask, he told himself. Better not to hear her spell it out.

"I have to. I appreciate what you've offered me, Kel." The words seemed to be difficult to get out. "Marriage and everything." She gestured vaguely to encompass the house and the ranch. "But I don't think we'd suit," she finished weakly.

"Seems to me we suit pretty well."

"In bed. But that's not all there is to marriage."

"We haven't done all that poorly outside of bed, either." But she was already shaking her head.

"Sooner or later, you'd realize what a mistake you'd made."

"Why don't you let me worry about that?"

"I can't," she whispered. "I can't let you worry about it. I have to think about Michael, too."

"You think our getting married would be bad for Michael?" Why didn't she just spit out the truth, that she didn't love him, would never love him.

"In the long run." Megan turned away and began putting things into the suitcase again. "When he realizes that you married me because you thought it was your duty, your *responsibility*."

"Most women would appreciate the fact that I want to live up to my responsibilities," he said, aware that his voice had risen.

"Your responsibilities?" She seized on the two words, making them less than a compliment. "You mean like it was Kurt Anderson's *responsibility* to marry Melissa?"

"Who?" Kel stared at her blankly, trying to figure out how Kurt and Melissa Anderson figured into the conversation. "What are you talking about?"

"Kurt and Melissa," she said impatiently. "She got pregnant and it was his responsibility to marry her. Remember?"

"I remember. What does that have to do with us?"

"They got a divorce, right?"

"Yeah. So what?"

"So I'm not putting myself or Michael through that," she said adamantly.

Kel stared at her, trying to piece together what she meant, which he suspected had little to do with what she was saying. Her eyes met his for a moment, then she turned and began throwing things into the suitcase again. She was really going to go.

Panic shot through him. He was across the room before he knew what he intended, picking up the suitcase and upending it on the bed, dumping everything out of it and then tossing the empty case on the other side of the bed, out of her reach.

"Stop the damned packing and talk to me."

"Why?" She offered not a word of protest but simply started to walk around him to get the suitcase. Kel grabbed her arms, holding her in front him.

"Just because Melissa and Kurt Anderson couldn't make their marriage work, it doesn't mean that the same thing will happen to us."

"Why wouldn't it?"

"Why would it? Damn it, Megan, you're acting like it's a foregone conclusion. Why won't you give it a chance?"

She was silent for so long that he thought she was going to ignore the question, but she finally lifted her head and looked at him. Her eyes were bright with tears but they were steady, seeming to look into his soul.

"I won't be a responsibility for anyone ever again. And I won't let Michael be one, either."

Kel stared at her, feeling as if he'd missed another piece of the conversation. "If we were married, you'd both be my responsibilities," he said slowly, trying to feel his way. "You're already my responsibility. Why is that such a bad thing?" He tried a half smile, trying to coax a lightening of her expression. But she continued to look at him with those lost eyes.

"When I was six, I heard my parents arguing about which one of them had to take me when they got a divorce. I can remember hearing them argue about whose responsibility I was. My mother lost the argument and I lived with her for a couple of years but then she met a man who wanted to show her the world." She was speaking rapidly but without inflection, as if she was reciting a familiar, not too interesting story. "Only he didn't want to show it to a kid. So she dumped me on my grandparents and they took care of me because it was the right thing to do, because it wouldn't be fair to turn the responsibility for me over to the state."

She stopped speaking, her eyes seeing past him to memories he couldn't share. Kel had no trouble imagining how devastating it must have been to spend your childhood knowing that you were being cared for out of duty rather than love. At least he'd had his father, and no one who knew Patrick Bryan had ever doubted his love for his children.

"I won't ever be anybody's responsibility again," Megan said flatly, shaking herself out of her memories.

"It wouldn't be just that," Kel said, searching for the words to tell her that responsibility wasn't all he felt. "I care for you."

He immediately cursed himself for the stupidity of that statement. Of all the yuppified, pantywaist phrases, that had to be the worst.

Megan seemed to agree, because other than a lift of her eyebrows, she didn't respond. She pulled loose from his slackened hold and walked around him. Picking up the suitcase, she put it on the bed and began heaping things into it.

He was going to lose her. If he couldn't get past his own demons and say the words she needed to hear, she was going to leave and take Michael with her. Oh, she wouldn't try to keep him away from his son. She'd be generous with visitation rights. But he didn't want visitation rights with Michael. He wanted him here, on the ranch, where he belonged. And he wanted Megan here, too.

"Don't go."

"I won't try to keep Michael from you," she said, stuffing a pair of shoes into the suitcase on top of a blouse. He saw something fall on the bright silk fabric and realized that she'd started to cry. The sad splotch of dampness gave him hope. "You're his father and you should be part of his—"

"I love you."

"—life. We'll work out something—"

"I said, I love you."

"—out." Her hands were shaking so much that she gave up trying to fold a pair of jeans and simply jammed them into one corner of the suitcase.

"Damn it, Megan. I'm telling you I love you." Kel's voice stopped just short of a roar.

"I heard you," she whispered. She leaned her hands on the edge of the suitcase, her head bowed and her shoulders hunched. "Thank you, Kel."

"Thank you?" He stared at her downbent head in disbelief. "I tell you I love you and you say thank you?"

"I know what you're trying to do. You're trying to make it easier for me. I—"

"I'm trying to make it easier for me." He came around the foot of the bed and caught hold of her shoulders, dragging her around to face him. The tears streaming down her face were nearly his undoing.

"Don't, Kel. Please. I know you're trying to do what's right, trying to live up to your responsibilities but—"

"To hell with my responsibilities," he snapped, but his hands moved gently on her shoulders. "This isn't about responsibility, Megan. I do feel responsible for you and for Michael. I'd be a pretty poor excuse for a man if I didn't. But I want you to marry me because I love you. I love you." Funny how the words got easier to say with each repetition. He smiled at her. "I love you."

She stared at him and he thought he saw a glimmer of hope in her eyes. "You can't."

"Why not?"

"Because . . . because it would be too perfect," she finished in a whisper.

"What's wrong with perfection?" He was suddenly feeling almost lighthearted.

"Are you sure?"

"I've never been more sure of anything in my life. I love you."

"Oh." That one little exclamation seemed to say it all. He could see belief sliding into her eyes. She set her hands on his chest and leaned forward until she could rest her cheek over his heart.

Kel slid his arms around her, drawing her close, savoring the feel of her against him, savoring the thought that she was his—this time forever. He bent to rest his cheek against the top of her head.

"Don't you have something to say to me?" he murmured, wanting to hear the words, even though he'd already seen the answer in her eyes, felt it in the soft curve of her body.

"I love you," she said softly, completing his world with that single phrase and all the promise it held.

* * * * *

continues...

Once again Rachel Lee invites readers to
explore the wild Western terrain of Conard
County, Wyoming, to meet the men and
women whose lives unfold on the land they hold
dear—and whose loves touch our hearts with
their searing intensity. Join this award-winning
author as she reaches the POINT OF NO RETURN,
IM #566, coming to you in May.

For years, Marge Tate had safeguarded her
painful secret from her husband, Nate. Then
the past caught up with her in the guise of a
youthful stranger, signaling an end to her
silence—and perhaps the end to her fairy-tale
marriage.... Look for their story, only from
Silhouette Intimate Moments.

And if you missed any of the other Conard County tales, you can order them now by
sending your name, address, zip or postal code, along with a check or money order
(please do not send cash) for $3.50 for each book ordered, plus 75¢ postage and
handling ($1.00 in Canada), payable to Silhouette Books, to:

In the U.S.	In Canada
Silhouette Books	Silhouette Books
3010 Walden Ave.	P. O. Box 636
P. O. Box 9077	Fort Erie, Ontario
Buffalo, NY 14269-9077	L2A 5X3

Please specify book title(s) with your order.
Canadian residents add applicable federal and provincial taxes.

CON6

HE'S AN

AMERICAN HERO

He's a man's man, and every woman's dream. Strong, sensitive and so irresistible—he's an American Hero.

For April: KEEPER, by Patricia Gardner Evans: From the moment Cleese Starrett encountered Laurel Drew fishing in his river, he was hooked. But reeling in this lovely lady might prove harder than he thought.

For May: MICHAEL'S FATHER, by Dallas Schulze: Kel Bryan needed a housekeeper—fast. And Megan Roarke did more than fit the bill; she fit snugly into his open arms. Then she told him her news....

For June: SIMPLE GIFTS, by Kathleen Korbel: For too long Rock O'Connor had fought the good fight to no avail. Then Lee Kendall entered his jaded world, her zest for life rekindling his former passion—as well as a new one.

AMERICAN HEROES: Men who give all they've got for their country, their work—the women they love.

Only from

INDULGE A LITTLE 6947 SWEEPSTAKES
NO PURCHASE NECESSARY

HERE'S HOW THE SWEEPSTAKES WORKS:
The Harlequin Reader Service shipments for January, February and March 1994 will
contain, respectively, coupons for entry into three prize drawings: a trip for two to
San Francisco, an Alaskan cruise for two and a trip for two to Hawaii. To be eligible for
any drawing using an Entry Coupon, simply complete and mail according to
directions.

There is no obligation to continue as a Reader Service subscriber to enter and be
eligible for any prize drawing. You may also enter any drawing by hand printing your
name and address on a 3" x 5" card and the destination of the prize you wish that entry
to be considered for (i.e., San Francisco trip, Alaskan cruise or Hawaiian trip). Send
your 3" x 5" entries to: Indulge a Little 6947 Sweepstakes, c/o Prize Destination you
wish that entry to be considered for, P.O. Box 1315, Buffalo, NY 14269-1315, U.S.A.
or Indulge a Little 6947 Sweepstakes, P.O. Box 610, Fort Erie, Ontario L2A 5X3,
Canada.

To be eligible for the San Francisco trip, entries must be received by 4/30/94; for the
Alaskan cruise, 5/31/94; and the Hawaiian trip, 6/30/94. No responsibility is assumed
for lost, late or misdirected mail. Sweepstakes open to residents of the U.S. (except
Puerto Rico) and Canada, 18 years of age or older. All applicable laws and regulations
apply. Sweepstakes void wherever prohibited.

For a copy of the Official Rules, send a self-addressed, stamped envelope (WA
residents need not affix return postage) to: Indulge a Little 6947 Rules, P.O. Box
4631, Blair, NE 68009, U.S.A.

INDR93

INDULGE A LITTLE 6947 SWEEPSTAKES
NO PURCHASE NECESSARY

HERE'S HOW THE SWEEPSTAKES WORKS:
The Harlequin Reader Service shipments for January, February and March 1994 will
contain, respectively, coupons for entry into three prize drawings: a trip for two to
San Francisco, an Alaskan cruise for two and a trip for two to Hawaii. To be eligible for
any drawing using an Entry Coupon, simply complete and mail according to
directions.

There is no obligation to continue as a Reader Service subscriber to enter and be
eligible for any prize drawing. You may also enter any drawing by hand printing your
name and address on a 3" x 5" card and the destination of the prize you wish that entry
to be considered for (i.e., San Francisco trip, Alaskan cruise or Hawaiian trip). Send
your 3" x 5" entries to: Indulge a Little 6947 Sweepstakes, c/o Prize Destination you
wish that entry to be considered for, P.O. Box 1315, Buffalo, NY 14269-1315, U.S.A.
or Indulge a Little 6947 Sweepstakes, P.O. Box 610, Fort Erie, Ontario L2A 5X3,
Canada.

To be eligible for the San Francisco trip, entries must be received by 4/30/94; for the
Alaskan cruise, 5/31/94; and the Hawaiian trip, 6/30/94. No responsibility is assumed
for lost, late or misdirected mail. Sweepstakes open to residents of the U.S. (except
Puerto Rico) and Canada, 18 years of age or older. All applicable laws and regulations
apply. Sweepstakes void wherever prohibited.

For a copy of the Official Rules, send a self-addressed, stamped envelope (WA
residents need not affix return postage) to: Indulge a Little 6947 Rules, P.O. Box
4631, Blair, NE 68009, U.S.A.

INDR93

INDULGE A LITTLE
SWEEPSTAKES

OFFICIAL ENTRY COUPON

This entry must be received by: MAY 31, 1994
This month's winner will be notified by: JUNE 15, 1994
Trip must be taken between: JULY 31, 1994-JULY 31, 1995

YES, I want to win the Alaskan Cruise vacation for two. I understand that the prize includes round-trip airfare, one-week cruise including private cabin, all meals and pocket money as revealed on the "wallet" scratch-off card.

Name_____

Address _____ Apt. _____

City_____

State/Prov._____ Zip/Postal Code_____

Daytime phone number_____
                                    (Area Code)

Account #_____

Return entries with invoice in envelope provided. Each book in this shipment has two entry coupons—and the more coupons you enter, the better your chances of winning!
© 1993 HARLEQUIN ENTERPRISES LTD.   MONTH2

INDULGE A LITTLE
SWEEPSTAKES

OFFICIAL ENTRY COUPON

This entry must be received by: MAY 31, 1994
This month's winner will be notified by: JUNE 15, 1994
Trip must be taken between: JULY 31, 1994-JULY 31, 1995

YES, I want to win the Alaskan Cruise vacation for two. I understand that the prize includes round-trip airfare, one-week cruise including private cabin, all meals and pocket money as revealed on the "wallet" scratch-off card.

Name_____

Address _____ Apt. _____

City_____

State/Prov._____ Zip/Postal Code_____

Daytime phone number_____
                                    (Area Code)

Account #_____

Return entries with invoice in envelope provided. Each book in this shipment has two entry coupons—and the more coupons you enter, the better your chances of winning!
© 1993 HARLEQUIN ENTERPRISES LTD.   MONTH2